"Miss Darcy!
lying out in

"Who?"

"I couldn't tell. It's too dark. I think it's a woman. I tried to help her up but she won't move."

As Tess came into the foyer, Lida appeared on the stairs. "What's going on?"

"Evidently we have somebody lying in the backyard. I'm going out to see what's

JEAN HAGER

WEIGH DEAD

AN IRIS HOUSE B&B MYSTERY

AVON BOOKS, INC.
1350 Avenue of the Americas
New York, New York 10019

Copyright © 1999 by Jean Hager
Inside cover author photo by Teresa Salgado
Published by arrangement with the author
Library of Congress Catalog Card Number: 99-94457
ISBN: 0-380-80375-5
www.avonbooks.com/twilight

First Avon Twilight Printing: November 1999

AVON TWILIGHT TRADEMARK REG. U.S. PAT. OFF. AND IN OTHER COUNTRIES, MARCA REGISTRADA, HECHO EN U.S.A.

Printed in the U.S.A.

WCD 10 9 8 7 6 5 4 3 2 1

Chapter 1

"Not a pretty sight," she muttered as she gazed at herself in the white-and-gold framed mirror.

Or rather at Pat Snell.

Pat Snell, Pat Snell, she repeated in her mind, trying to embed the name so deeply that she wouldn't make a telling slip. Such a slip could cost her everything. Everything that mattered, at any rate.

The blue eyes of the woman looking back at her gazed through new horn-rimmed eyeglasses—with lenses that turned sunglass-brown when she was in the sun. She had never worn glasses before, and they had already rubbed a tender spot on one side of her nose. She massaged the spot with her index finger for a moment, then removed the glasses and studied her face—short nose, wide mouth, smooth skin thanks to a laser peel, and perfect white teeth thanks to modern dentistry. The hair made a difference, but perhaps not enough. Better keep the glasses. With a sigh, she put them back on.

She picked up her brush and ran it through her short, dyed black hair one more time. It did not magically transform her reflection into Sandra Bullock, more's the pity. She turned her head sideways to examine her profile. She *did* have a nice profile when she was thirty pounds lighter and that little lump of fat under her chin was gone.

1

Sighing, she tossed the brush aside and smoothed both hands down ample hips to press the wrinkles out of the green cotton slacks she'd bought in a Chicago discount store. The slacks had elastic at the waist to accommodate her thick middle. The tails of her white shirt hung down over the slacks, a pathetic attempt to hide the bulge of her stomach. She looked like some middle-aged house-wife who'd had three or four kids and then just gave up the fight and let herself go to hell.

In contrast to the woman in the mirror, the room re-flected behind her was daintily feminine—lace ruffles, white wicker, and spring green and lavender chintz. A framed watercolor of the ruffled lavender iris for which the room was named hung over the delicately scrolled white-and-brass iron bed. Even the view from the win-dow overlooking the big front yard—clumps of daffodils hugging a white wrought-iron fence—seemed designed to complement her accommodations.

The Annabel Jane Room in Iris House Bed and Break-fast was light and airy and quite lovely. When she'd checked in, she'd been pleasantly surprised to find she would be spending the next two weeks in such charming surroundings. Unfortunately Pat Snell looked as out of place there as a fat English bulldog at a Yorkshire Ter-rier show.

Dr. Patrice Singleton, on the other hand, would be right at home. But Dr. Patrice had perfectly styled, frosted blond hair and a trim, fit body—and no patience with those who let themselves go, like Pat Snell. Dr. Patrice bought her designer clothes at Saks Fifth Ave-nue. She wouldn't be caught dead in the getup worn by Pat Snell, or any of the other discount shirts or slacks and shorts, with elasticized waists, hanging in the closet of the Annabel Jane Room. Furthermore, if Dr. Patrice needed corrective lenses, she'd wear contacts. No, she'd get that laser surgery. Dr. Patrice did not readily tolerate human imperfections.

But Dr. Patrice was on an extended vacation in the Caribbean. She had not told anyone, not even her boss at the Chicago radio station that syndicated her call-in show, how she could be reached, saying she simply must have some uninterrupted time away from her grueling schedule. Time to think and plan the agenda for the fall shows, which were organized around a different theme each week.

She *had* told him that when she returned, she'd be a brand-new woman. He hadn't mentioned her weight gain, but she'd caught him studying her figure when he thought she wasn't looking.

However, knowing that she had a lucrative offer from another syndicate, he'd indulged her. Besides, she had enough tapes in the can to cover three months, if necessary.

For the next two weeks, while Dr. Patrice lolled in the sun, Pat Snell would spend the time at Iris House in a weight-loss retreat conducted by Lida Darnell, the woman who owned Lida's Fitness World in Victoria Springs. Pat Snell had three months to take off thirty pounds, and she was determined to shed the first ten before the retreat ended. Lida's two-week makeover package carried a hefty price tag, but if it worked, it was well worth it. Not *if*, she told herself. It *would* work.

Pat Snell would probably sign up for another weight-loss program after this one. She knew she couldn't come out of the next three months thirty pounds lighter without a rigid structure and somebody to tell her what to eat and when. The bald truth was that Pat Snell was so undisciplined, she needed a keeper.

She was seriously considering getting counseling. There had to be somebody somewhere who could help her keep the weight off once she lost it.

Dr. Patrice, of course, would shake her head in disgust at such weakness. But she was Pat Snell for now and money was no barrier. Whatever it took, she had to get the weight off by the first of June. Otherwise Dr. Patrice was finished. Besides which, the thought of traveling around the country in her current revolting condition made her want to crawl under a bed.

Her stomach grumbled. Denied her late-evening bowl of Ben & Jerry's Heath Bar Crunch ice cream the pre-

vious day, Pat was hungry enough to eat the ivy flowing
from a wicker basket near the lace-curtained south window. Unhappily, there was the morning jog to get
through before she could eat.

Her mind still on food, she turned away from the mirror, wondering what the cook was serving for breakfast
which, combined with lunch, could contain no more than
six hundred calories. They would go out for dinner so
that Lida could teach them how to order five-hundred-
calorie meals from a menu. Lida had explained all this
to her when she'd arrived at Iris House last evening.

She had also been asked to sign a release giving Lida
and her trainer, a Tom Cruise look-alike, permission to
conduct random searches of her room and luggage for
contraband food.

Shades of all those summer camps she'd attended as
a child!

She had instinctively bristled at the invasion of privacy, but had stifled the impulse to voice her outrage—a
typical Dr. Patrice reaction—and signed on the dotted
line.

What choice did she have?

She was up against the wall, but she had always managed to come through when faced with a deadline. With
the help of Lida and the trainer she would do it again.

The trainer was named, to her disbelief, Cail, and he
had so many muscles, his muscles had muscles. He must
spend a couple of hours a day working out with weights;
the very idea made her shudder. And the thought of the
muscular, cocky Cail rifling through her belongings, especially her large size 10 underpants made her skin
crawl. The man had shifty eyes. Handsome as he was,
there was something almost unsavory about Cail Marrs.

Get over it, she told herself as she headed for the door.

"It's exactly what you deserve for having so little self-
control," she lectured. "Behave like a child, without restraint, and you deserve to be treated like a child. Where
did you think all those desserts would go, anyway?"

That sounded exactly like Dr. Patrice. She paused at
the door to gather her wits and take a deep breath.

"Pat Snell, Pat Snell, Pat Snell," she murmured as she left the room.

Still in her robe, Tess Darcy dashed out to the Iris House veranda for the morning paper. As she returned to her apartment via the foyer, Pat Snell, one of the guests who'd checked in last evening, came down the stairs.

Tess paused in her open doorway to say, "Good morning, Pat."

Pat peered at her over the top of her eyeglasses as she came down the last few steps. "Oh, hi. Is breakfast ready yet?"

"I think you're the first one down," Tess said, "but Gertie will serve you in the dining room whenever you're ready."

Pat pushed her glasses up to the bridge of her nose, then immediately readjusted them to rest halfway down her nose. "I was ready an hour ago. I'm hungry enough to eat the furniture. I hope whatever's on the menu is filling."

Tess didn't have the heart to tell her that the two hundred calories allotted for breakfast by Lida Darnell, the woman running the retreat, would probably not allow for a meal that could honestly be described as filling. Gertie was the best cook in Victoria Springs, Missouri, but she couldn't work miracles.

"By the way," Tess said, "when you checked in, I gave you a form to fill out. You left the blank form in my office. If you'll wait just a minute, I'll get it for you." Before Pat could reply, Tess stepped into her apartment, dropped the morning paper on the sofa, and returned to the foyer with the form.

Pat took it, scanned it, and handed it back. "I'm a very private person. I don't like the idea of my home address and phone number lying around in somebody's files."

"Oh." Tess was taken aback. Nobody had ever reacted quite that way to the simple form. "It's just that I usually mail thank-you notes after guests return home. And sometimes I send former guests announcements of special events scheduled in the area. Several have returned for a second visit after receiving the mailings."

Pat had the closed expression of someone who's mind is already made up and nothing anyone says will change it.

"But, of course, if you'd rather not . . ."

"I'd rather not," Pat said flatly.

Tess forced a smile. "Fine. Now, I'd better get dressed. I'll see you later." Closing her apartment door behind her, Tess thought, *How strange.* Since Pat had given her a down payment in cash it wasn't essential that Tess have her address and phone number. But she did find Pat's response intriguing.

And Pat wasn't the only current guest who had aroused Tess's curiosity. In fact, some of the undercurrents she'd picked up already were a bit worrisome. One guest, a high-fashion model known professionally as merely Lillith, had arrived with an obese husband and heavy-set adolescent boy whom Tess had surmised was the model's stepson. When Tess had observed casually that Lillith didn't look as if she needed to lose weight, the woman frowned, gave a quick shake of her head, and rushed her family up the stairs, away from Tess. Another young woman named Heather had quizzed Tess about Cail Marrs, the trainer who would be working with the group. How long had he lived in Victoria Springs? What was his relationship with Lida Darnell, his employer? *Odd questions to ask about a stranger*, Tess had thought. But when she inquired if her guest knew Cail, Heather had hastily changed the subject. Later, after she'd shown Heather to her room, two sisters, who were sharing accommodations, had arrived in the midst of a heated argument. Tess hadn't learned what the dispute was about, but the older of the two had called her sister a brainless nitwit, to which the younger had replied that she, at least, had more in her life than work. It made Tess wonder how they would manage to spend two weeks in the same room without coming to blows.

Shaking her head, Tess went to get dressed. She had a feeling the next two weeks would provide some surprises.

Chapter 2

Rudy Hansel gaped at his beautiful second wife, stunned into momentary silence. Her shining red hair was done up in a French braid, and the white shorts and navy T-shirt set off her tall, lithe figure to perfection. She was the most beautiful woman he'd ever seen, and he still marveled daily that this picture of female perfection could be his wife. At the moment, though, he was not in a marveling mood.

He struggled to lever his bulk off the quilted, coral sofa in the Darcy Flame Suite, almost toppling a black-laquered Chinese folding screen in the process. Lillith caught the screen—which was decorated with hand-painted coral and blue lilies—with one perfectly manicured hand.

Finally getting his feet under him, Rudy steadied himself by planting one hand on the arm of the sofa and waved the flyer she'd just handed him under her nose. "Lillith," he gasped, "tell me this is a joke."

"Now, calm down, sweetie," Lillith cooed. "Remember your blood pressure."

"Screw my blood pressure!"

"Rudy, you *said* I could plan our vacation and surprise you—anywhere I wanted to go, you said, anything I wanted to do."

"This is no vacation! It's a concentration camp. How could you do this behind my back?"

"Because I knew you'd never agree to it up front. It's for your own good, dearest. Yours and Kent's."

Rudy's twelve-year-old son, Kent, chose that lamentable moment to emerge from the bathroom. He looked suspiciously from his father to his stepmother. "What's for my good?"

"The next two weeks, Kent," Lillith told him. "You'll both thank me when it's over. Trust me on this."

Kent was not yet as overweight as his father, but he was getting there fast. "After what's over?" he asked, scowling at his father. "We're on vacation, aren't we? Dad, you promised we could go to that video game arcade we saw in town right after breakfast." He licked his lips as a slightly glazed look slid over his round face. "I hope we're having waffles."

He'd find out soon enough that there would be no waffles for the next two weeks. "I'm afraid there won't be time for video games, dear," Lillith said, reaching out to smooth the boy's brown hair, still damp from the shower, off his forehead.

Kent jerked away from her touch. "Dad promised!"

Lillith pretended not to notice the dislike in Kent's eyes. He still resented her for marrying his father a year ago. Rudy had indulged him shamelessly since his mother's death. Lillith hoped that during the next two weeks, she could break down some of the barriers Kent had erected against her, something she'd been trying to accomplish for months with little success. If she failed, the boy could make her life hell.

"He made the promise before he knew how full our schedule here would be," Lillith said with great patience. "You'll have to give up your video games for two weeks. There won't be much time for watching television, either. We're going to be involved in other activities—doing things together as a family."

"What activities?" Kent demanded.

With a flourish, Rudy unfolded the flyer still clutched in his beefy hand and read, "Walking, running, aerobics, weight-lifting, group support sessions. Oh, yes, and we'll do all this on eleven hundred calories a day."

"Twelve hundred," Lillith corrected him. "Men and adolescents get twelve hundred calories a day."

"Well, praise God!" Rudy responded sarcastically.

Kent pointed an accusing finger at Lillith. "She *tricked* us, Dad! She's always trying to change us. Mom never did that. Mom loved us just the way we are."

And nearly killed you with fat-laden food, Lillith thought. But she knew better than to voice the slightest criticism of the first Mrs. Hansel, who'd been plump and retiring and, as far as Lillith could learn, had rarely had an opinion of her own. Since her death, however, she had attained the status of a saint in her son's eyes.

"Dad!" Kent whined. "I don't want to stay here. We don't have to, do we?"

"Why don't you wait for us downstairs, Kent," Lillith said quietly, but there was steel under the words.

The boy set his jaw, looked at her mulishly, then glared at his father. "Do we?"

Rudy took a deep breath, tugged his white terry-cloth robe back together in front, and flopped down on the couch. "Go on, son. We'll be along in a minute."

"Why does *she* always get her way?" Kent muttered mutinously.

"Kent," said Rudy sternly. Kent sighed and left.

As soon as the door closed behind Kent, Lillith sat down next to her husband and stroked his thick thigh with a slim hand. "Don't be mad at me, honey. And please don't oppose me in front of Kent. Remember, we talked about how important it is to always present a united front to him, no matter how much we disagree in private."

"I didn't mean to start an argument in front of Kent but, damn it, Lillith, this has taken me by surprise."

"I know, dear, but try to cooperate, please. I had hoped we could grow closer together as a family during the retreat."

Rudy clutched his balding gray head. "While starving to death? Good thinking, Lillith."

"You won't starve." Lillith smiled indulgently. "After the first couple of days, you'll actually have more energy, and you'll see that eating the proper kinds of low-calorie food will satisfy you."

"Right. I suppose you mean lettuce and carrot sticks and that other stuff you live on."

"Foods with fiber stay with you longer. As a model, I had to learn to eat right, Rudy. You get used to it. Once it's a habit, you don't even feel deprived."

His eyes remained skeptical. Clearly he didn't believe a word of what she'd said. "Well, I'm never going to be a model and neither is Kent. And if you ask me, you could afford to put on a few pounds, not lose more."

Lillith knew he didn't really mean that. He was always telling her that she had a perfect body. "I probably won't lose a pound, Rudy. I rarely consume more than eleven hundred calories a day, anyway." Her fingers tightened a little on his thigh. "Listen to me, sweetie. If you won't do this for yourself, do it for your son. Kent has no friends at school. He's too heavy and out of shape to do well at sports. You know how cruel kids can be. They make fun of him, call him Fat Albert."

Rudy looked pained. "How do you know that? Kent never mentioned it to me."

"I heard one of his classmates call him that when I picked him up at school."

"Which one?" Rudy demanded. "I'll have a word with that kid's parents."

"That would only make it worse for Kent. And don't ask him, either. It would be humiliating for him to have to talk to you about it."

"Maybe you're right." He heaved a deep sigh.

Lillith went on. "The rest of Kent's school days will be miserable if he doesn't take off some weight. Don't you want to help him fit in?"

Rudy slumped back on the couch. "You're very good at switching things around so I'm the one on the defensive, Lillith, but Kent's fitting in is not really the point here—"

There was a tap at the door. Lillith jumped up to admit

the handsome young trainer they'd been introduced to last night. He'd flirted with her shamelessly behind Rudy's back. She had not been impressed. Lillith had had her fill of handsome men; most of the ones she'd known—admittedly male models—were so self-centered they assumed the mere privilege of being in their company was all any woman could possibly expect of them. She'd put the trainer in the same category on sight.

With some difficulty she dredged up the trainer's name from memory. Cail Marrs.

Cail appraised her appreciatively. He grinned, reminding Lillith of a wolf, dark eyes deep set, hair a glossy black. "Good morning, Mrs. Hansel."

"Good morning, Cail."

He continued to give her that intent, meaningful look, his handsome face tilted, a faint smile on his sensually carved lips. He was issuing an invitation or a challenge; she wasn't sure which. In either case, she wasn't having any.

"May I come in?"

Lillith stepped back. Cail entered, nodded at Rudy, went immediately to the closet, and began rummaging through pockets and shoe boxes.

Rudy's jaw dropped. He lumbered up off the couch and plowed across the room. The front of his robe had come loose again, and it flapped around him like the wings of a giant duck trying to get airborne after a heavy meal. "Get away from there! What the hell do you think you're doing?"

The back of Cail's neck reddened. Slowly, he turned around. "I'm doing my job, Mr. Hansel," he said reasonably.

Lillith grabbed hold of her husband's arm. "He's conducting a random search, darling. It's in the contract I signed."

Cail held up two Snickers candy bars—king size. "Candy is not allowed, Mr. Hansel," he said with an apologetic smile as his eyes slid over Rudy's stomach which protruded over his boxer shorts, exposed by the open robe. Then he gave Lillith another wolfish grin accompanied by a sympathetic shake of his head, as if to say she'd gotten her husband there just in time.

"Get out of here, you muscle-bound steroid freak!" Rudy roared, waving his arms.

Cail's smile slipped as his prominent brow bunched tightly into a frown.

"You'd better go, Cail," Lillith said hastily.

Hands clenched, he hesitated. Then, he seemed to shake himself and, unclenching his hands, he made a wide circle around Rudy and left the room.

"That's it!" Rudy yelled as the door closed behind Cail. "We're out of here."

"No, Rudy," Lillith wailed. She took his round face in her hands and kissed his flushed cheek. "I did this because I love you. I want to keep you with me for years and years. You know the doctor said that weighing so much is dangerous. Your cholesterol is already higher than a kite. If I lose you, they might as well rip my heart out."

"Don't be so dramatic, Lillith. There would be men on your doorstep before my body was cold."

"But I don't want other men. I want you. Please, just try it for a couple of days. For me. Please."

He had never denied her anything when she pleaded and said she loved him. For an instant, it looked as if this might be the first time. He pulled away from her touch and went to the window, turning his back. Lillith knew when she'd said enough. She waited.

At length, he turned around. "I'll reevaluate the situation in two days, Lillith." His words were clipped, his tone brooked no argument, as if he were addressing a group of subordinates in the company boardroom of his real estate empire. His decisiveness was one of the things she loved about him—but not in this particular instance. "Whatever I decide at that time is the way it will be. Agreed?"

Lillith released a relieved breath. She had two days to bring him around. "Whatever you say, sweetie."

"But Pretty Boy better keep his distance. I saw the

way he looked at you. And if he or that Lida woman ever step foot in this suite again while we're here, I won't be responsible for my actions."

"Yes, darling. I'll talk to them." She would have to promise to search Rudy's and Kent's belongings herself. If Lida wanted them to stay, she'd go along with it. And Lillith was sure she wanted them to stay; if they left, Rudy would certainly demand a refund of their hefty registration fees. "I think it's about time for our morning run."

"Run! You want me to keel over with a heart attack?"

"You're right, dear. We'll just walk briskly." Her tone was chirpy, conciliatory. "I'm sure there will be others who aren't ready to start running yet."

"Exercising before breakfast! It's barbaric."

"It'll be fun on such a beautiful day. You'll see. Oh, and you might want to put on your walking shorts and those new cross-trainers I bought for you. Lida and Cail will be waiting."

He went to the closet and tore a huge pair of shorts from a hanger. "Damned diet Nazis," he muttered as he began to dress.

Chapter 3

Next door in the Carnaby Room, Heather Brackland heard the Hansels leave the suite and walk toward the stairs. Lillith's light step was a counterpoint to Rudy's heavy tread, like grace notes fluttering against the background of a thumping bass drum.

Heather had checked into Iris House last night as the Hansels were being given their key. Tess Darcy had introduced them, then they had excused themselves to go upstairs. She'd immediately recognized the beautiful former model and her multimillionaire husband. Every important paper in the country had carried the story of the widowed real estate tycoon's engagement, three years after his wife's death, to one of the best-known supermodels in the world. A few weeks later, Lillith had announced her retirement from modeling, saying that she planned to concentrate full-time on making a home for Rudy and his son. "I never knew I could love like this," Lillith had been quoted as saying. "Rudy is everything I ever wanted in a man."

Yeah, right, Heather thought. *The fact that the fat slob was worth millions didn't hurt, either.*

Last year, the tabloid Heather worked for, *The National Scoop*, had run her two-page spread of the Hansels's wedding in the garden of Rudy's country estate. She'd snapped some great shots of the cer-

15

emony while hanging by a strap out the open door of a helicopter. Rudy Hansel had threatened to sue the tabloid, but they received such threats all the time, and nothing had come of Hansel's posturing.

Fortunately the Hansels didn't know her on sight and they had not appeared to recognize her name when she was introduced. Ever on the lookout for a story, Heather had already phoned to ask that the tabloid's file on the Hansels be e-mailed to her as a text file. She had also requested that the research department dig up anything else they could find on Lillith and Rudy. *Turn over every rock*, was the way she'd phrased it.

Heather never went anywhere without her laptop and her camera. Fortunately, she'd have a good excuse for snapping shots of the Hansels. She'd suggested to Lida that her clients might like before and after pictures of themselves, and Lida had gone for the idea.

The Hansels's attendance at a weight-loss retreat was a gift; it would make a decent story—not sensational, but good enough for a filler. The headline might read: BEAUTIFUL MODEL TELLS HUBBY, GET THIN OR GET OUT!

The important thing was that doing the story would provide Heather with a semivalid excuse for being there herself. Of course, if she was backed into a corner, she would never admit that she was focusing on the Hansels; she'd just say she was doing a story on weight-loss programs.

Not that she couldn't afford to lose a few pounds, but she'd never have shelled out the money for such a top-dollar program for that reason. All she had to do to drop ten pounds was give up sugar for a few weeks. No, the opportunity to lose weight was not why she'd maxed out her VISA card to come to the retreat.

She was there to confront Cail. Although she hadn't seen him when she checked in, he had to know she was registered. He had probably never expected she'd go to so much trouble to find him, even though they'd bought a condo together in L.A. and he'd left her holding the bag—rather, the mortgage payments—when he disappeared without a word.

Well, Cail was about to find out that nobody did a number like that on Heather Brackland and got off scot-free. She smiled as she imagined the shock he must have felt when he saw her name on the list of registrants. She had another little surprise for him, too, which she would reveal at the most strategic moment.

"Pay-up time, Cail," she murmured, as she sat on the four-poster bed to put on her new Nike running shoes.

After tying the laces, she flopped back on the bed and gazed up at the white canopy. While on the trail of stories, she'd been inside some of the most elegant hotels in L.A.; nevertheless, she was still impressed by Iris House. Her room, named for the Carnaby iris, was decorated in shades of soft blue, white, and rose, the color of the iris depicted in a painting on the wall. The room's wallpaper and matching ruffled draperies were splashed with rose, pink, and blue tulips. The overall effect was incredibly romantic. Unfortunately, the last thing she expected during her stay was romance.

She closed her eyes and thought about Cail, the man she'd loved to desperation. Still loved, she acknowledged when she was being perfectly honest with herself. But Cail's desertion had spread a layer of disillusionment and anger over the love, convincing her it really was true that there was a fine line between love and hate. Now she wasn't sure how she would feel when she saw Cail again.

Which would probably be within the next few minutes. He and Lida were scheduled to lead the group in a run—or walk, for those who weren't fit enough to run—before breakfast.

She stood and checked her appearance once more in the dresser mirror. She'd had several sessions in a tanning booth before leaving L.A., and the tan looked good with her yellow knit shirt and Spandex running tights. Her ash-blond hair was held back with a yellow elastic loop. With the tan, her face looked healthy without makeup, which would be a waste of time if they were going to run first thing.

Heather tried to make the best of what she'd been

born with, but she knew she wasn't beautiful. That's why she'd felt so lucky to be with utterly handsome Cail. She'd loved the way other women had looked at her enviously whenever they went out together.

And when he left her, she could read people's reactions on their faces: *A good-looking man like that . . . he was bound to leave her sooner or later. It's a wonder it lasted as long as it did.*

She'd told everyone the breakup had been mutual. Things were getting too serious, and neither of them was ready to settle down. They needed space to think. She doubted many people believed her, but they'd had the decency to keep their opinions to themselves.

She closed her eyes for a moment, picturing Cail's face, the way his mouth curled up on one corner when he grinned, the cleft in his chin. The face of a Greek god, but when he was angry, the same eyes that went all soft and unfocused when they made love could turn as hard as granite. Though he had never physically abused her, that look was frightening enough.

Oh, Lord, could she really do this?

For a brief moment, she was tempted to send word that she was too ill to come downstairs this morning. But the moment passed. She'd have to show her face eventually. Better to get the first meeting over with.

She lifted her chin. So, she wasn't beautiful, but she wasn't exactly the Bride of Frankenstein either. And she sure wasn't going to be any man's doormat.

She felt a rush of the bulldog determination that filled her whenever she was on the trail of a good story, the feeling that she could overthrow any obstacle placed in her path. She was here to make Cail take responsibility for the mess he'd made of her life and, by God, nothing was going to stop her.

Chapter 4

In the Arctic Fancy Room, Marcia Yoder stood, buck naked, at the window. Stretching like a cat, arms extended, she caroled, "Such a beautiful day, and that gorgeous yard! I love this place. The atmosphere is so conducive to spiritual regeneration. I must call Ahmed and tell him all about it."

Dorinda Fenster, Marcia's sister and ten years her senior, stomped out of the bathroom in her new cotton knit shorts, T-shirt, and running shoes. She frowned in disgust at Marcia's broad backside, where she stored most of her excess weight. "For God's sake, Marcia, cover your butt or get away from the window. Somebody will see you."

The sisters were sharing the Arctic Fancy Room for the two-week retreat. Dorinda hadn't come to lose weight, though five pounds less on her sturdy, compact body would be nice. She'd come to keep an eye on her sister, who'd gone absolutely crazy since she'd been dumped, after twelve years of marriage, by her dentist husband, who'd moved in with his twenty-year-old receptionist.

Marcia had immediately thrown herself into affairs with questionable men, a couple of whom had had no visible means of support and had looked and acted like gangsters. Marcia had even started to sound like them, talking about "the family" or saying somebody was "connected." Marcia had always been too easily influenced by whoever her current companions were. It had gotten her into several tight spots, which Dorinda had had to get her out of.

Dorinda understood about the affairs, though. Her sister had been trying to prove that there *were* men in the world who wanted her, even if her husband didn't. But understanding didn't quell her disgust with Marcia. Dorinda didn't suffer fools gladly.

Recently Marcia had dropped the gangster types and gotten involved with some shyster guru from Sri Lanka who advocated "getting in touch with the natural world, freeing the inner self, and being completely honest in all things," which apparently included parading around in broad daylight in one's birthday suit. Dorinda knew that this Ahmed's little group of followers—mostly females— often celebrated their "freedom" by dancing nude out of doors at midnight. "Communing with the night," Marcia called it. Dorinda called it Ahmed's sly way of surrounding his lascivious little self with naked women.

She hadn't dared let Marcia spend two weeks at the retreat alone. No telling what she might get involved in if Dorinda weren't there to rein her in. She'd probably have ended up in jail—or a psych ward—for exposing herself in public. Dorinda wasn't absolutely certain she could prevent a disaster, even while on the scene. She couldn't watch her sister every minute. She would just have to be the voice of reason whenever an opportunity presented itself.

It was a shame she couldn't use these two weeks to relax, go for long walks alone, and read a couple of novels, things she rarely had time for back home. The Arctic Fancy Room, with its deep violets, blues, and whites, would be such a soothing retreat in other circumstances. In other words, without her flighty, wide-load of a sister to supervise.

"Marcia!" Dorinda snapped.

Finally, her sister turned from the window to face her. Her hazel eyes narrowed, indicating deep thought, not an easy task for Marcia. Their mother had always said that Dorinda got the brains and Marcia got the looks. As

a teenager, Dorinda had been devastated by such remarks. As an adult, she thanked her lucky stars she
wasn't in Marcia's shoes.

"Don't be such a puritan, Dorinda," Marcia said. "I
know you're a big corporate lawyer, but there's more to
life than business suits and courtrooms and legal briefs.
That stuff's not real. At best, it's playing a role and,
more often than not, it's deceitful and dishonest." Her
well-endowed bosom quivered. "That's why nobody
trusts lawyers."

"Who told you that, the white-robed one?"

"Go ahead, make fun of me. I don't care." She tugged
irritably on a strand of mud-colored hair which she'd
recently had clipped pixie-style. The cut might have
looked cute on a teenager, but it did nothing for Marcia's
longish chin. "You've never really understood me, anyway."

That was true enough. "I've tried, believe me," Dorinda muttered.

"No, you've tried to change me. There's a difference.
I don't want to hurt your feelings, Dorinda. I'm just
being honest. Ahmed says we must turn our backs on
everything false. We must make amends for every
wrong we ever did and every lie we ever told if we're
to be truly happy. Honesty purifies the soul."

Did her ditsy sister even know what she was saying?
"That's ridiculous. What are you going to do, find every
grammar school kid you ever fibbed to and apologize?"

For an instant Marcia chewed her bottom lip and
seemed to consider it. "You're so bottled up, Dorinda.
You might as well be wearing one of those nineteenth-
century corsets that made women faint all the time."

"I never wore a corset in my life."

"It's a figure of speech. Really, you should take a
good, honest look at yourself—if that is even possible
after so many years practicing law. You should get in
touch with the real you. I think you'd find recording
your thoughts in a journal a big help." At Ahmed's urging, Marcia wrote long frequent journal entries, evidently recording whatever floated through her muddled

mind. "What I'm saying," Marcia went on, "is you have to learn to live a freer life."

"By running around with my tush hanging out? I don't think so, thank you very much."

Marcia frowned sadly. "Don't be ashamed of your body, Dorinda. It's beautiful. All human bodies are beautiful. No matter what the shape or size."

"Then why did you drag us here to lose weight?" Which Dorinda was paying for, by the way.

"Our bodies are the vessels for our spirits. If we love our vessels, we'll take care of them."

"Oh, spare me your Ahmed quotes."

Marcia tilted her head and studied her sister with slitted eyes. It made Dorinda nervous when Marcia got that look. It meant she was up to something stupid. It would be far easier if she could simply disengage from Marcia until she got her head together again, but she'd taken care of her sister since their parents were killed when a truck hit the family car broadside. Marcia and Dorinda had miraculously escaped with a couple of broken bones, but their parents, who'd been seated on the side the truck hit, had died instantly. Marcia had been only twelve at the time, and Dorinda, who'd entered law school the following fall, thanks to a settlement from the trucking company's insurance carrier, had brought her sister to live with her in an apartment near the University of Texas campus in Austin.

Even after Marcia married, she'd come to Dorinda with her problems and Dorinda had always risen to the occasion. She'd even represented Marcia in her divorce, had tracked down the dentist's hidden bank accounts, and managed to get a good chunk of money for her sister. Left alone, Marcia would have let the scum walk off with everything. Not that Marcia had handled the money sensibly. Dorinda was sure most of it was gone by now.

Taking care of her sister was a habit Dorinda couldn't seem to break.

"Hadn't you better get dressed if we're going on that run? Or do you plan to dash through town naked, with your boobs bouncing all over the place? If that's the case, perhaps we should rent a horse."

Marcia shrugged and reached for the underwear she'd tossed on the bed. "The time will come when we can do away with clothes altogether." She frowned at her white panties with distaste. "We won't need nudist camps because the whole world will be one."

Dorinda gave a helpless shake of her head. "Do you really believe that?"

"Of course. Ahmed says clothing is just another way for the dishonesty establishment to restrain and control us. They hide their ugliness under cotton and silk."

Dorinda snorted. "That makes about as much sense as the other things Ahmed says."

Marcia wriggled into her panties, reached for her bra, and went on talking as if Dorinda hadn't spoken. "The whole fashion industry is a big con, and what's worse, it's built on slave labor. There's a high-fashion model staying here right now—Lillith. That's her professional name, just Lillith, no last name. As if she's so important everybody will know who Lillith is."

"Almost everybody does," Dorinda said dryly.

Marcia shrugged that off. "Just wait. You'll see how self-satisfied and arrogant she is."

Dorinda laughed in spite of herself. "How can you say that? You don't even know this woman."

Marcia lifted her shoulders carelessly. "Models. They all think they're God's gift."

"That's a generality that wouldn't hold up on close scrutiny, I'm sure."

Marcia ignored her sister's statement to continue with her opinion. "The time will come when all the designers and models will be exposed for the shallow, soulless people they really are."

When Marcia got on her soapbox, reason was wasted on her. Dorinda had heard quite enough.

"I'll wait for you downstairs."

Chapter 5

Tess Darcy lingered for one last look out her sitting room window. For once, the huge daffodils along the front fence had sent up their green shoots, formed tender buds, and bloomed without a late February frost nipping them before the petals had a chance to unfurl and reach for the sky. The daffodils were the first bloomers of the various flowers planted in beds around Iris House, bright yellow harbingers of spring that gave Tess a lift every time she saw them.

With a contented sigh, she turned from the window and left her apartment. After one step into the stone-floored foyer, however, she halted, hearing a tense male voice coming from the guest parlor.

"What the hell are you doing here, Heather?"

"Why, Cail! Hello. Imagine meeting you in Missouri, of all places. Small world, isn't it?"

"Answer my question. What are you up to?"

"If you must know, I'm researching weight-loss programs for a story I'm writing. But what are *you* doing here?"

"I *live* in Victoria Springs." Cail's voice was taut with restrained anger. "I work for Lida Darnell, the woman who's running this retreat."

"Really?"

"Drop the innocent act. Don't try to tell me you didn't already know I worked for Lida."

Heather uttered a nervous little laugh. "How could I? You disappeared from L.A. without a word, not even good-bye."

"I knew you'd make a big scene. Women always do when a guy wants out."

"Poor Cail, I suppose that happens to you frequently. How awful for you, to be subjected to such unpleasantness. But you didn't even leave a forwarding address with the post office. One would almost think you didn't want to be found."

"You should have taken the hint."

"The point is, I had no way of knowing you were here. I certainly didn't recognize the name Cail Marrs on the brochure Lida sent me."

"Listen, Heather." His low tone held an edge of menace. "Lida is considering taking me on as a partner. If you mess that up . . . in fact, if you breathe a single negative word about me to Lida—"

"Are you threatening me?"

"I'm giving you some advice. Lida and I—"

"Oh, Lord, don't tell me!" Heather interrupted. "I know by the way you say her name. You're up to your old tricks. You're sleeping with her, aren't you?" She uttered a brittle laugh. "Sleeping your way to the top. Before I met you, I always thought that was a female ploy."

"My relationship with Lida is none of your damned business!"

"Oh, Cail, is there nothing too low for you to stoop to? The woman has to be ten or twelve years older than you—at least. Does she know how casually you can walk away from your responsibilities?"

"I'm warning you, Heather, don't try to cause trouble for me with Lida."

"That will be up to you."

"What does that mean?"

"Figure it out," Heather snapped. "Cail Hurst or Cail Marrs or whatever you're calling yourself these days."

The exchange was getting too heated for Tess to remain silent any longer. She reached back to ease open her apartment door, then slammed it, clearing her throat loudly to announce her presence, and continued across the foyer to the guest parlor.

"Hello, Heather. Cail." When her guests checked in, she established immediately whether they preferred being called by their first or last names. She always asked to be called Tess, and usually they followed suit.

" 'Lo, Tess," Cail replied shortly and, with a venomous glance at Heather, he left the parlor via the foyer. Opening the front door, he stepped out onto the veranda, where several guests already waited.

Heather watched him go, her eyes fixed on the door through which Cail had disappeared. She was as tense as a tightly curled spring.

"Are you all right, Heather?" Tess asked.

"What?" She tore her gaze from the door and swiveled her head to look at Tess. She took a deep breath. Her eyes were troubled. "Oh, yes, I'm fine," she said and followed Cail outside.

If ever Tess had seen anyone who was *not* fine, it was Heather. She stood there a moment, pondering what she'd heard. It seemed clear the two had a history together. And Heather had called him Cail Hurst. Naturally curious, Tess wondered what that meant and how she could find out.

Shaking her head, she went to the kitchen where Gertie Bogart, the Iris House cook, was preparing breakfast. Nedra Yates, the housekeeper, sat at the round oak table, eating a bowl of raisin bran drowned in half-and-half— her usual breakfast. Her bucket of cleaning supplies sat on the floor near the door to the dining room.

Gertie stood at the center work island measuring skim milk into small, individual pitchers. As usual, she wore a billowing tent dress—this one was lime green—with a bibbed apron tied around her ample waist. Like many good cooks, Gertie enjoyed her own creations a little too much. She'd even self-published a cookbook of her recipes, which continued to do a brisk business in Victoria Springs's gift shops and at the Queen Street Book Shop, which was owned by Tess's cousin Cinny Forrest.

"Good morning," Tess greeted them as she lifted a mug from the rack and poured herself a cup of coffee. "What's for breakfast?"

Gertie's disgusted glance slid in Tess's direction. "For us or the guests?" she asked.

"The guests."

"Half cup of bran flakes, half cup of skim milk, and half cup of fresh strawberries, if you can call that breakfast." Gertie's lips twisted wryly. "I'll tell you the truth, Tess. I've always been proud of what came out of this kitchen—until now."

When Lida Darnell had reserved the whole of Iris House for the first two weeks in March, she had arranged to pay Gertie extra to prepare lunch as well as breakfast for the guests. The two meals combined were to contain no more than six hundred calories—seven hundred for men and adolescents.

Gertie had muttered and complained for days that it was not only impossible, but downright cruel. Then Lida had brought over a stack of low-calorie, low-fat cookbooks and finally Gertie had settled down, filled the refrigerator with fresh fruits and vegetables, and come up with two weeks' worth of menus. "Meals for birdies and emaciated women like Lida Darnell," Gertie had called them.

Now Gertie said, as if it were a personal affront, "I've been ordered to lock up the sugar for the duration."

"Tell you where it is, Tess," Nedra said. The housekeeper had a habit of starting to talk in the middle of a thought, but Tess had learned to interpret Nedra-speak pretty well.

Gertie translated, anyway. "She means we'll tell you where to find the key to that corner cabinet—where the sugar is." She glanced toward the dining room and lowered her voice. "The key's taped to the bottom of the silverware drawer."

"Silly," was Nedra's comment. She wore her usual work uniform—jeans and a cotton shirt, her flyaway, straw-colored hair held back with a pink headband.

"Stupid, too," Gertie added. "If they want sugar, they can buy some in town."

"They won't have much time to slip off to town," Tess said. "Lida showed me their schedule. Except for a short break in the morning and another in the afternoon, there's something going on all day, every day, including Saturday and Sunday. In addition to the benefits of exercising and support sessions, keeping busy is supposed to divert their minds from food."

"Speaking of exercise, Lida left a bunch of dumbbells in the parlor," Gertie said. "All sizes."

"They're using the parlor for weight-lifting and aerobics," Tess told her, "with all the furniture pushed back against the walls."

"Well, I'm not moving any furniture. Period," Gertie stated.

"The guests will do that," Tess said. "Good exercise, according to Lida."

Gertie rolled her eyes. "Help us all. That woman is obsessed with exercise. Can't be still a minute. Makes a body tired just to watch her."

Tess nodded, wishing she had Lida's seemingly unending store of energy. She went to the refrigerator and took out a big basket of strawberries. She spooned some into a small bowl, sliced in a banana, and retrieved the key to the corner cabinet. It was secured to the silverware drawer with wide masking tape. She sprinkled a couple of spoonfuls of sugar on her fruit, returned the sugar canister to its shelf, snapped the padlock closed, and retaped the key to the drawer.

"People weren't meant to weigh all their lives what they weighed at sixteen," Gertie was muttering. "It's unnatural." The cook had never been on a diet in her life and had said more than once that she never intended to be.

Chuckling to herself, Tess carried her breakfast to the table. As she sat down, Lida Darnell hurried into the room. Tess thought her black shorts and striped tank top looked a bit scanty for the first of March. The temperature might hit seventy later in the day, but right now it was two or three degrees below fifty.

Lida came to a stop and began to bounce on her athletic shoes, as if she'd built up too much momentum on her way there to stand still. "Contraband," she announced, holding up two candy bars. "May I stash these in your freezer?"

"Help yourself," Tess told her.

Lida's eager feet took her to the adjoining utility room, where she lifted the lid of the chest-type freezer and tossed in the candy. Coming back into the kitchen, she said, "Should the person who brought the candy go in search of it, he'll have time to change his mind about eating it—while it's thawing out."

In spite of Gertie's opinion, Lida wasn't emaciated. She was very thin, but her legs and arms were firm with running and weight-lifting muscles. Since she'd called the candy sneak "he," it had to be Rudy and/or Kent Hansel. Tess pictured Lida wresting the candy from their plump grasps and wished she could have witnessed it.

"We're off on our run," Lida said. "Should be back in thirty or forty minutes—or a few of us should be. I swear, some of those people are physical wrecks. It will take more than two weeks to get them in shape. Did you see that Hansel boy? It's a crime to let a child get in such a condition. Oh, well." She bounced out of the room, stopping in the dining room to pick up the bathroom scales she'd left there.

"Poor little boy," Gertie whispered.

"Kent Hansel, you mean?" Tess asked.

Gertie nodded. "I'll bet coming here was all that skinny stepmother's idea."

Tess thought she was probably right, but she could understand Lillith's motives. Rudy Hansel looked like a stroke waiting to happen. And Kent was too heavy to enjoy many of the activities of most twelve-year-olds. It was about time somebody took them in hand.

Nedra stood and picked up her bucket. "—follow me around a while, wouldn't need to run," she said, as she trudged off.

"Nedra's got a point," Gertie said.

But Tess suspected the housekeeper's bony figure had more to do with metabolism than her housekeeping chores.

In the foyer, Lida opened the front door and called, "Okay, troops, we'll weigh in and stretch out before we go."

In the kitchen, Gertie muttered, "Lida should be a drill sergeant, the kind that persecutes green boys through boot camp."

On the veranda, Lida continued getting her charges organized. Pointing to her left, she announced, "Heather has kindly agreed to take before and after pictures of you."

"Nobody's taking my picture," Pat Snell protested loudly. "And I'm not getting weighed in front of everybody, either."

"I'll turn the scales so nobody can see but you and me," Lida assured her. "I want a record of your beginning weight in your folder. The files are private. Nobody will see yours but the two of us. We won't weigh again until the last day. I don't want you obsessing on numbers." She raised her voice to an even louder pitch. "Kent, lose the jacket. You won't need that much clothing."

Kent whined something that sounded like, "I'm cold."

"Not for long. We'll get your blood circulating. Oh, and Pat, I hope you'll change your mind about the picture. I think you'll be pleased with how much better you look in just two weeks."

"No picture," Pat repeated loudly and firmly.

"Well, whatever . . ." Lida sounded exasperated. She closed the door and kept on talking, but Tess could no longer understand the words. From a front window, she watched Lida record the guests' weights as each one stepped on the scales. As they stepped off, Heather snapped a picture. She even took a shot of Pat Snell when Pat was looking the other way.

Some minutes later, as the guests were leaving, Tess heard a vehicle stop out front. "That must be Wayne

Armory," she said. Wayne was in charge of constructing an addition to Iris House, where Tess and Luke Fredrik would live after their marriage in June.

"Sounds like he needs a muffler," Gertie observed.

"I'd better go remind him not to let his workers start before eight. All the guests should be up by then." Later she might have to ask them to wait until nine, in deference to future guests.

"Could be a problem, anyway," Gertie said. "There won't be much peace and quiet around here for a while."

"I'll tell potential guests about the construction before they make reservations, so they can make other arrangements if they want." Tess stepped into the utility room, grabbed a windbreaker off a hook, and put it on over her red jumpsuit.

As she stepped onto the veranda, Wayne Armory was getting out of his pickup. His son Donnie, a freckle-faced, string bean of a boy of eleven or twelve, was with him.

"Hi, you two," Tess called.

"Hey, Tess," Wayne responded. He stood, looking toward the retreating backs of Rudy and Kent Hansel, who brought up the rear of Lida's little group. Those in front were running, putting distance between themselves and the walkers.

Just before the group turned a corner and were lost from sight, Lillith slowed down until she was walking beside Rudy. She was saying something, probably encouraging her husband and stepson to pick up the pace. Kent looked down at his shoes as though he didn't want to hear it.

"Looks like Lida's got her work cut out for her with some of those people," Wayne observed.

"Yes, indeed, but if anybody can shape them up, it's Lida." Tess smiled at Donnie. "Who's your helper, Wayne?"

"Donnie's going to lend me a hand this week. School's out for spring break." Donnie's mother worked in a local bank, so evidently it was up to Wayne to keep the boy occupied when classes weren't in session. Having no children of her own, Tess didn't keep up with the school schedule.

"I hope you're making him pay you, Donnie."

"He's getting a regular apprentice's wages," Wayne said, with a broad wink for Tess. "Two dollars a day and lunch."

A second pickup pulled in behind Wayne's and two men in khaki shirts and overalls got out. Neither of them looked to Tess to be over thirty. They waved at Wayne and nodded politely to Tess as they passed.

"I wanted to remind you," Tess said to Wayne, "not to start hammering or anything noisy like that before eight." She feared the crew might decide to put in some early overtime since Luke had added a bonus clause to the contract if the job was finished by June first.

"I already told the men," Wayne said, "but I'll remind them again. I know you've got a houseful of guests to consider. And after Lida gets through with them, they'll need a good night's rest." He turned to Donnie. "Son, you better start getting the tools out of the truck. We'll be digging the foundation footings today."

"Donnie," Tess said as he turned away. "There's a twelve-year-old boy staying here. If he has any free time, I'm sure he'd like to meet you."

Donnie perked up at the prospect. "Okay. Cool." He walked to the back of the pickup, pulled out two shovels, and started dragging them across the yard.

"Way to go, Donnie!" one of the young workmen yelled. "You're the man!"

"Well, I won't keep you, Wayne." Tess would have enjoyed standing there indefinitely, picturing Iris House with the new addition and dreaming about living there with Luke.

But duty called.

Chapter 6

Tess was in the kitchen, having a second cup of coffee, when the guests began to return. Rudy and Kent Hansel were the last to straggle in. As they climbed the stairs, she heard Kent say, "I hope we're having waffles."

"Banish the thought, son," Rudy replied. "We're on a diet, remember?"

Cail used the downstairs bathroom to wash up and change clothes. Although Lida had checked into the Black Swan Room for the retreat, Cail was not staying at Iris House. He occupied an apartment at the fitness center.

When Cail came out of the bathroom wearing a tight black T-shirt and shorts, rippling muscles looking as if they would burst through the fabric any minute, he found Lida in the dining room setting a stack of books on the table. He pulled her aside. "There's something I need to warn you about," he said.

Tess didn't hear the rest, except once when Lida cried, "Stalking you!" He shushed her and they finished the conversation in whispers.

Tess busied herself filling the silver coffee urn and teapot while questions circled through her mind. Was Cail talking to Lida about Heather, saying that Heather had stalked him in L.A. and had now tracked him to Victoria Springs? If so, was that true or just a story made up for Lida's benefit? Tess realized that she thought Cail would lie if it served his purposes. For one thing, nothing had been said about stalking in the conversation between Cail and Heather which Tess had overheard earlier. For another, there was something about Cail's manner at times that made him seem less than trustworthy, though Tess could not quite put her finger on what it was.

She was setting the coffee urn and teapot on the dining room buffet when the other guests started coming downstairs. In spite of being the last to return from the run, Rudy and Kent, accompanied by Lillith, were first at the table. Cail and Lida, having finished their conversation, came in from the parlor. Shortly, Heather Brackland, Marcia and Dorinda, and Pat Snell joined the group. The women's faces were still rosy from exertion.

Gertie served in silence, clearly not pleased to be responsible for the scanty offerings she set before them. Since Rudy and Kent were entitled to extra calories, they got orance juice. The others had a choice of coffee or tea without sugar or cream and six ounces of tomato juice.

Kent stared aghast into his cereal bowl, then glared at Gertie. "Hey, lady, I want waffles."

Gertie squinted down at him, planting one hand on her hip. "You can take that up with Lida, young man. I just work here." She finished serving and retired to the kitchen.

"Miss Darcy," Kent said, sounding plaintive now, "can I have some sugar?"

Fortunately Lida spoke up, saving Tess the necessity of replying. "Sugar is poison, Kent. It's also addictive." She stood to pull several blue paper packets from her shorts pocket and tossed them on the table. "If you must have sweetener, use this. One should do. You won't know the difference."

"Is this all we get to eat?" Kent asked.

"You'll get used to it," Lida told him.

"But I'm starving!"

"Eat slowly," Lillith advised. "It'll make you feel fuller."

"Nothing would make me feel full," Rudy complained, "except maybe a couple of fried eggs, bacon, and biscuits."

"With strawberry jam," Kent added wistfully.

Lida dismissed the complaints by changing the subject. "I've brought copies of Dr. Patrice Singleton's last book, *Lose the Fat, Get a Life*. I want you to read the first two chapters during our morning break. We'll discuss them after lunch."

"I just love Dr. Patrice," Lillith said. "I heard she'll be touring with her new book this summer."

Rudy picked up the book on top of the stack and opened it to the back cover flap. He stared glumly at the photograph of Dr. Patrice. "Isn't this that hard-nosed bitch who's on the radio?"

Lida's sharp nose quivered with disapproval. "She's the best known fitness and nutrition expert in the country," she informed him, "probably in the world."

Rudy swiped tiredly at his perspiring face with a handkerchief, still looking at the photograph. "She's an attractive woman, but hard as nails." He glanced up at Lida. "Have you heard the way she talks to people who call in to her show? They're already feeling as low as a snake's belly and are looking for a little support to help them lose weight and she cuts them down. Doesn't want to hear about your metabolism or your thyroid . . ." His voice went up an octave and became more nasal as he mimicked Dr. Patrice. "You got yourself into this mess. You chose to be fat. You can just as easily choose to be thin and fit."

Sitting at the kitchen work island, Tess could see most of the table. Now she observed that Pat Snell was engrossed in adding sweetener to her tea. She saw, too, how Lida's lips thinned to a hard line of determination. "She doesn't let people get away with excuses," Lida said, her voice strained with quickly intensifying impatience. "She's just trying to make them take responsibility for their actions."

"So you're big on taking responsibility for your actions, are you, Lida?" Heather inserted, looking straight at Cail, whose mouth formed an oval, then clamped shut.

Lida looked puzzled. "Of course."

Heather studied her for an instant, as though she were a rare bug viewed through a microscope, then gave an indifferent shrug. "Dr. Patrice is probably one of those people who can eat anything and never gain a pound. Lucky genes."

"Luck has nothing to do with it," Lida snapped. "Unless you mean the kind of luck you make for yourself."

Tess happened to be looking at Heather at that moment and she saw the slow, deliberating stare Heather gave Lida. After an instant, Heather said, "Not necessarily. Unless you live alone on a desert island, you have little control over many of the things that happen to you."

Then Heather stared straight at Cail, whose color turned brick red. He lowered his head.

"Sometimes," Heather went on, "other people—irresponsible people—come into your life and bring you bad luck."

Lida's questioning eyes darted from Cail to Heather. "Are we still talking about diet and fitness?"

Heather held her gaze for a long moment. "Of course we are," she said with a faint sneer.

Lida flexed her fingers as though she'd like to use them to scratch Heather's face. Then she dropped her hands to her lap and scanned the other faces around the table, skipping over Heather's, as though dismissing an ugly stain on the tablecloth. "During the next two weeks, you will learn how to live with three sensible meals a day and no snacking in between. You'll learn to listen to your body and let it tell you when you're hungry. If you feel truly hungry between meals, there will always be celery and carrot sticks and some cans of tomato juice in the refrigerator. You can have all you want of those."

Heather seemed not to be listening, for suddenly she said, "Pat, you look familiar to me. Have we met before?"

"No," Pat said shortly.

"Have you ever been to L.A.?"

"Nope."

"Where do you live?"

"Kansas. I operate a craft mall in Topeka—one of those places where crafters rent booths to display their wares."

Heather nodded thoughtfully, then lowered her gaze. The guests finished their breakfast in glum silence. Tess noticed that not a single strawberry or flake of cereal was left.

Finally Lida said, "Let's go into the parlor now for our group session." Under her guidance, they arranged sofa, loveseat, and chairs in a semicircle. Once they were seated, Tess helped Gertie clear the table.

Lida continued to hold forth. "Following our discussion, Cail will lead our aerobics session. I've brought some great tapes for us to exercise to." She smiled brightly around the semicircle, eliciting a few tentative smiles in return.

Kent, who was seated next to the dining room door, muttered, "Aerobics is girl stuff."

Heather, sitting beside him, said, "No it isn't. I take aerobics in L.A. and there are several men in the class. Some of them are real macho guys, too."

Kent shot her a dubious glance. "You're just saying that to make me feel better."

Heather laughed. "No, I'm not. Why should I care how you feel?"

Kent stared at her, his mouth ajar. Clearly he was not accustomed to being told his feelings were not relevant.

"I don't suppose," Marcia ventured, "we will be allowed to exercise in the nude."

Everyone swung to look at her. A giggle erupted from Lillith.

"For God's sake, Marcia!" Dorinda groaned.

"Clothes are so restraining," Marcia said.

Gertie and Tess had retired to the kitchen, where Gertie turned from the cookbook she was leafing through to gaze at Tess, her sandy brows lifted in amazement.

In the parlor, Lida was trying to deal with Marcia's unusual request as best she could. "Er . . . no. Are you forgetting there will be men and a child present?"

Kent spoke up, his round face creased in an indignant scowl. "I'm not a child." But he was watching Marcia with great interest now.

"Young man, then," Lida amended.

"We should stop teaching our children to be ashamed of their bodies," Marcia said primly.

Kent frowned again at the "children," but before he could protest, Lida did. "Could we save that discussion for another time?" she asked wearily, going on before Marcia had a chance to reply. "Now then, let's talk about why we eat."

Downcast, Marcia slumped back in her chair while her sister glared daggers at her.

"Because we're hungry," Kent responded to Lida.

"That's one reason, Kent, but be honest. Don't we all eat sometimes when we aren't hungry?"

"I eat when I'm bored or depressed," Heather offered.

Pat nodded. "So do I. And when I'm worried. Most of all when I'm under stress."

Heather snorted. "You don't know what stress is, running a craft mall in Kansas. You should try being a reporter in L.A."

Rudy's head swiveled around like a turtle coming out of its shell.

"Boredom, depression, stress," Lida put in hastily, trying to keep the discussion on track. "These are all common reasons for overeating. We must learn to substitute something else for food at those times—like a long walk, or a shopping trip, perhaps for something we've been wanting a long time. It doesn't have to be anything expensive. Buying a little gift for yourself will lift your spirits."

Rudy was still studying Heather. "What kind of reporter did you say you are?"

Heather gnawed the inside of her cheek, as if she wished she could call back her last words. "I'm a stringer for a small weekly. Just a community newspaper. You wouldn't have heard of it."

Cail, who up till now hadn't spoken since breakfast, growled, "She's lying."

Every head in the room turned toward him, faces registering surprise. Lida appeared dumbfounded. "Cail . . ."

Cail ignored her and went on. "Heather works for *The National Scoop*. It's a scandal sheet. No reputable journalist would have anything to do with it."

Heather's look was hot enough to start a campfire. "Who are you, Mr. *Marrs*, the final authority on what is reputable? Don't make me laugh."

Cail's jaw hardened. Heather addressed Rudy. "I *am* a stringer for a community paper. I also take an occasional assignment from *The Scoop*. I can't afford not to. I have to work for a living."

"She told me she's doing a story on weight-loss programs," Cail expanded with seeming relish.

"Mr. Hur—oh, excuse me, Mr. Marrs is mistaken."

Cail's expression was pugnacious. "She told me so herself."

"I meant it might make an interesting story, but I haven't run it by my editor yet."

Lida was looking thunderstruck. "Heather, I hope you're not here under false pretenses, because if you are—"

Heather interrupted. "I'm here to lose weight like everybody else. A story might or might not materialize from the experience. If so, it would certainly have a positive slant."

"Hah!" snorted Cail. "*The Scoop* wouldn't recognize a positive slant if it fell over it. And if *that* happened, they'd run like hell the other way."

Lida did not seem convinced either, and she opened her mouth to say something else, but Rudy interrupted her, his face registering comprehension. "Wait a minute!" he slapped his knee. "Heather Brackland. I knew I'd heard that name before. You wrote that story on my wedding. You took pictures from a helicopter. The noise almost ruined the ceremony."

Now they were all staring at Heather with distaste.

Lida looked as if she wanted to wring her hands. "Could we get back to our discussion?"

Rudy ignored her. "Heather, I want those pictures you took today of me and my family. The negatives, too."

"I'll get the pictures—and the negatives," Lida said grimly. "Heather will turn them over. Right, Heather?"

Heather shrugged. "Sure."

"What's to stop her from getting two copies of the pictures?" Rudy demanded.

"I'll handle it," Lida snapped. "Leave it to me, Mr. Hansel."

Rudy leaned around his wife and stuck a finger in Heather's face, his eyes fixed on her with sheer hatred. "If one of those pictures, if even a single word about me or my wife or son appears in that supermarket rag again, I'll sue. I'm not bluffing this time. And if I see you taking any more pictures of us, I'll smash the damned camera."

Lillith tugged at her husband's arm. "Don't upset yourself, dear."

He shook off her hand. "I'm sick of these sleazy parasites who make their living feeding on other people's lives. They ought to all be lined up and shot!"

Lida jumped to her feet. "Mr. Hansel! That's enough. Drop it or excuse yourself."

Rudy's face swelled up like an angry bull's. "See here—"

Lida interrupted. "Whatever problem you have with Heather should be dealt with in private. You are wasting everyone else's time."

Red-faced, Rudy muttered an oath and stared at the floor. His clenched hands slowly loosened.

Lida waited a beat and went on, "And Heather, if I find out you *are* here to write an unflattering story, you will be asked to leave."

Heather gazed back at her with an indifferent expression.

"Now," Lida went on, "let's see if we can come up with other things we might do when our emotions tell us to eat."

"Anger must be one of those emotions," Rudy said, glaring at Heather, " 'cause right now I could eat a horse."

"Lillith," Lida said through gritted teeth, "as a model, you must have learned some tricks. Help us out here."

Lida managed to keep the discussion on the subject for the rest of the allotted time at the end of which she announced a ten-minute break before the aerobics session. She hurried from the parlor, looking drained, as if she'd been through a thirty-minute ordeal, instead of a support group meeting. Cail trotted after her.

The others filed out of the parlor behind Lida and Cail, heading for their rooms.

Heather hung back, letting the others go first. Pat Snell, the last in the line leaving the parlor, dropped back to say, "Heather, I don't appreciate your taking a picture of me when you thought I wasn't looking, after I asked you not to."

Heather looked at her for a long moment. "What's *your* problem?"

"I made myself very clear. No pictures."

"I don't get it. What're you in such a stew about?"

"I want the picture you took of me, along with the negative."

Heather threw up her hands. "You can have the stupid picture! What in the world would I do with a picture of a woman who runs a craft mall? Geez, you people are touchy. Give me a break, will you?" She stormed out of the room, almost knocking Pat aside as she brushed past her.

Pat grabbed hold of the door frame to steady herself. An angry pink flush spread over her face. For a moment, she stared after Heather. Then she took a step to follow her up the stairs, but stopped.

Turning back, she stared thoughtfully at the camera which Heather had left behind, tucked under her chair. Tess thought she seemed frozen there by indecision. She looked as if she were carrying on a silent argument with herself.

Then Pat started toward the camera, halted, and looked toward the foyer. Finally, she sent a furtive glance toward the kitchen and saw Tess watching her.

"Forget something, Pat?" Tess asked.

"No," she said and left the parlor.

Chapter 7

As soon as the parlor was empty of guests, Tess went to her apartment to catch up on her book-keeping. Since Luke had given her a laptop computer last Christmas, keeping up was much easier than it had been when she posted everything by hand to a ledger. Even though she'd been reluctant to join the computer world at first, she was glad Luke had persisted to the point of actually buying the computer and teaching her to use the book-keeping program he installed. The program was a scaled-down version of the one Luke and his assistant, Sidney Lawson, used in their financial management business.

The message light on her office telephone was blinking. She punched the "messages" button and heard Luke asking her to call him. She keyed in his office number which, for once, wasn't busy.

"It's me," she said when he picked up.

"Hi, honey."

"Is this a bad time for you to talk?"

"I can take a minute. It's good to hear your voice."

Luke's deep voice gave Tess a warm, snuggly feeling. She sighed happily into the sweet silence.

"How is Lida's retreat going?" Luke prompted.

"Okay, so far." Tess gave her mind a quick jerk to bring it back from wool-gathering. "I envy

Lida's organizational ability. She's got the retreat schedule down to the minute. Some of the guests are very
intriguing, too. It turns out one of them, Heather Brackland, works for *The National Scoop*."

"The what?"

"It's one of those supermarket tabloids you see by the
checkout stand."

"The ones with stories about people being kidnapped
by aliens or raised by wolves?"

"Exactly. Evidently she did a story on Rudy Hansel's
wedding, which he didn't appreciate. It came out in their
morning support session. Rudy was livid. Poor Lida had
a time getting them back to the discussion. She finally
had to ask Rudy to leave or shut up."

She heard Luke's deep chuckle. "You always have
such interesting guests, love. But I'm sure Lida can handle them."

"We'll see," Tess mused. "There's something going
on with Cail Marrs and Heather, too. I overheard a really
weird conversation between them this morning, and they
keep taking little digs at each other."

"Sounds like this Heather won't be voted Most Pop-
ular Girl at the retreat."

"That's a safe bet."

"Have Wayne Armory and his crew started work on
the addition yet?"

"They're digging the foundations as we speak. Oh,
Luke, I can't wait until our new home is ready to move
into. I can already picture us lounging on our patio on
summer evenings, discussing the day's events."

He made a rough sound, like the evil chortle of a
villain in a melodrama. "And it will be so conveniently
close to our bedroom, too."

"I'm sure you had that in mind when you planned it,
my darling."

"You know me so well," he said. "Want to go out to
dinner this evening?"

"Yes," Tess agreed enthusiastically. "There's so much
talk about food around here, I'm sure I'll be starved by
dinnertime. I'll probably be exhausted, too, because

Aunt Dahlia's picking me up at two and we're going to the country club to talk to the caterer about the reception. You know what a whirlwind my aunt can be. How do you feel about gladiolas? Or is that gladioli? Never mind. They aren't too funerally, are they?"

"Gladiolas are great. Whatever you want, sweetheart."

"Aunt Dahlia's insisting on having lots of flowers at the reception as well as the wedding." Dahlia Forrest, Cinny's mother, had announced that, as the Forrests' wedding gift, she would pay for all the flowers for Tess and Luke's big day.

"Let her go crazy. It'll make her happy."

"You know I couldn't stop her, even if I tried."

"That's true. Well, I'll pick you up at seven. Just a minute, hon. What's that Sidney?" He came back in a moment. "Have to go, Tess. One of our small cap stocks is making a move."

Whatever that means, Tess thought. "Later, love," she murmured as they hung up.

Before starting work on the books, she took a few moments to sit on the window seat beneath the bay window where Primrose, the gray Persian, whom she'd inherited with the house from her Aunt Iris, was napping. The cat opened one eye and looked up at her, then nudged Tess's hand with her nose. Stroking Primrose's head, she listened to the cat's loud purring and watched the workmen, who were digging where there had once been an iris bed.

Tess and her Aunt Dahlia had spent several days removing the irises from the bed and replanting them elsewhere in the big yard. Tess would lose the bay window when the addition was complete, as the office would be on an interior wall. But she would not lose the view since the north wall of the new master suite, which would be at the northeast corner of the house, would be almost entirely glass, with a door opening to a brick-paved patio. Also the new living and dining rooms would have windows on that side of the house. She loved her bay window, but giving it up was a small price to pay for what she was getting in return, the most important of which was Luke.

Her present living quarters would be incorporated into the addition, making a lovely home for her and Luke. Sometimes, she thought with a sigh of longing, it seemed that June would never arrive.

As soon as Heather Brackland reached her room after the group session, she logged on to her computer. As instructed, *The Scoop*'s research department had sent her the newspaper's files on the Hansels. Also, there was a second file containing other information the researcher had managed to uncover. She clicked on that file. The researcher had added a note at the beginning:

We called in some favors owed and got the following bombshell from one of our deep throats. Two bombshells, I should say. We're checking other sources now for hard evidence. Have fun!

Adrenaline surged through Heather and her reporter's heart hammered as she read the accompanying document. My God, two bombshells was right! This was great stuff. Did their source know what he was talking about? It couldn't have been easy to come by this information. But if there was hard evidence out there, the researcher would find it. The *Scoop* had a top-notch research department. They could almost always find where all the bodies were buried.

This was front-page stuff!

As Heather finished reading, she rubbed her hands together with glee. Two of the best stories of her career, and here she was in Podunk, Missouri. But she could e-mail the articles. She'd do the one on Rudy first and hope the research department came up with corroborative evidence. Even if they didn't, it wouldn't stop them from printing the story. Heather knew how to word it so that proving slander would be extremely difficult. She was tempted to start writing immediately, but when she looked at her watch, she saw that eight minutes of the break had passed. She'd have to work after dinner, staying up all night if necessary. It wouldn't be the first time. Reluctantly, she logged off and went downstairs.

Chapter 8

The aerobics class went off without a hitch, though Rudy and Lillith made it a point to position themselves as far from Heather as possible. Heather was not particularly offended. Once people found out she wrote for *The Scoop*, many of them went out of their way to avoid her. You'd think she had the plague or something, she told herself as she kicked in time with the music. She glanced at Rudy once, then had to look away to keep from laughing out loud. The tub of lard was sweating like a horse already, and they'd just started. What in the world did Lillith see in him? Besides the money, of course.

A more interesting question was: Did Lillith have any idea that the endless stream of dollars was in jeopardy? Probably not. Rudy was the kind of man who felt women needed to be protected from unpleasant financial facts.

After the aerobics session, they worked out for ten minutes with the dumbells, then were sent to their rooms with instructions to read the first two chapters of Dr. Patrice Singleton's book in the half hour that remained before lunch.

Heather darted out of the parlor and ran up the stairs. In her room, she hastily scanned the two chapters, then began work on the Rudy story. She felt superstitious about starting on the Lillith story until she had hard evidence—it sounded too incredible to be true. But if she could get some evidence, it was exactly the sort of gossip *The Scoop*'s readers loved.

The time passed too quickly, but she managed to write and polish the first two paragraphs. She printed them out for added insurance.

Then she found the invoice she'd prepared for Cail earlier, stuck it in her pocket, and began backing up her story to a disk.

Shortly before lunchtime, Tess found a stopping place in her bookkeeping and decided to go out and see what the construction crew had accomplished. As she stepped into the foyer, Kent Hansel came down the stairs.

"Have you finished the reading assignment already?" Tess asked.

"Naw. Dad's going to tell me what it says." He made a stab at looking pitiful. "It's hard to read when you're starving."

"Just fifteen minutes until lunch," Tess told him.

"If I live that long."

"How about some carrot sticks?"

Kent made a face. "No, thanks."

"Okay, then I have another idea. There's a boy about your age outside. His father's the foreman of the construction crew. Come along and I'll introduce you."

They found Donnie seated on the grass, going through his father's toolbox. Tess introduced the two boys, and Kent sat down next to Donnie.

"Where you from?" Donnie asked.

"We have four houses, but mostly we live in Orlando."

"Way cool! You get to go to Disney World any time you want to."

"It gets old after a while."

Donnie looked as if he couldn't imagine it.

"Say," Kent went on, "you wouldn't happen to have anything to eat, would you?"

"Just a snack my Mom packed—a couple of cookies, I think. We're going to town for lunch."

"A cookie would be great!"

Shaking her head, Tess walked over to speak to Wayne.

A few minutes before lunch, which according to Lida would feature "oven-fried chicken," Heather left her room with her book. The smell of the meat cooking made her mouth water. She stepped into the foyer, catching Cail in the act of passing through.

He glanced her way and his lips curled into a sneer before he reached for the doorknob. She stuck out her hand. "This is for you," she said.

He frowned at the piece of paper in her hand, but didn't reach for it.

"Take it, damn you." Heather spat the words. "Or I'll give it to Lida and ask her to pass it on."

He snatched the paper and unfolded it. "What the hell is this?"

"It's an invoice for your half of the last four mortgage payments on the condo."

"Thirty-two hundred dollars! You've got to be kidding." He tore the note in two and stuffed it in the pocket of his shorts.

"You owe me the money, Cail. I expect payment before I leave here and you will mail me a check for eight hundred every month thereafter."

He turned from the door and advanced on her. In spite of her determination to stand her ground, she took a step back. He grabbed her shoulders, gripping so hard she winced. "Read my lips. When I left, I left everything. The condo is yours. I'm not about to make payments on a place where I don't live."

She twisted in his grip. "Let me go." When his hands dropped, she went on, "You cosigned the mortgage. You own half of it."

"I'll sign it over to you."

"Your name will still be on the mortgage. And you know I can't qualify for the loan on my own. There's no way I can afford to make the full payment."

"Your financial problems are no business of mine,

Heather. You can always sell the damned condo and get a cheaper place."

"The real estate market is in a serious slump, or haven't you heard? I couldn't sell the condo now."

"That's *your* problem." He turned away.

"Cail!" Her shrill tone stopped him. "I want the money. If I don't get it, I can make big trouble for you."

"Don't try to bluff me, Heather."

"I don't bluff. You should know that!"

"What's your point?"

"The police paid me a visit after you left. What they had to say was quite interesting."

His steel-eyed stare made her want to back away even farther, but she didn't. If she appeared weak, she'd never get the money.

"If you want to play rough," he snarled, "I can get rougher."

She had seen Cail angry before, but never like this— with a murderous look in his eyes. It frightened her. But what could he do to her, really? If he got physical, she'd file charges and use his real name—or what she thought was his real name.

"If I don't get the money," she said between gritted teeth, "I'll contact the L.A. police. I'm sure they'd love to know where to find you. There are charges still hanging—something about the little sideline you had at the gym where you used to work."

He stared at her for a long moment, his eyes glittering with unadulterated hatred. "You bitch," he said in a soft but dangerous tone. Then he opened the front door and went out to the veranda, slamming the door behind him so hard the stained-glass panels rattled.

The silence left in his wake seemed to quiver with menace. Heather took a bracing breath, straightened her shoulders, and wiped her sweating palms on her shorts. She would *not* be intimidated.

She went into the parlor. She had thought the parlor was unoccupied, but Pat Snell sat slumped in an armchair, her head resting on the chair back, her eyes closed. *Pretending to be asleep*, Heather thought, but of course

Pat had probably heard every word Heather had exchanged with Cail. *Well, what of it?* Heather asked herself and tossed her head.

Pat's glasses rested on the table beside her chair. She didn't open her eyes as Heather walked over, picked up the glasses and tried them on. She was curious as to why Pat kept fiddling with them, as if the lens prescription was incorrect. Odd. Heather could see through the glasses just fine and her vision was 20/20. The lenses were clear glass. Now, why would anybody who didn't need corrective lenses wear glasses?

Pat stirred and opened her eyes. "Give me those!" she cried and snatched the glasses from Heather's hand. She put them on, pushing them into place with one finger on the nose piece. Then she opened her book and began to read, or pretended to, ignoring Heather.

What a loser, Heather thought, as she sat down in the same chair she'd occupied during the morning support session and opened her own book. But instead of reading, she studied Pat's profile, wondering why the woman seemed vaguely familiar. She was sure she'd seen her somewhere before, but it was hard to imagine where. Heather had never been to Topeka, Kansas, and Pat said she'd never been to L.A.

And why was Pat so adamant about not having her picture taken? Maybe she was just self-conscious about her weight.

Still, Heather thought, perhaps she should have the research department look into Pat Snell's background. Probably a waste of time, though. But wouldn't it be funny if they actually turned up a dark secret from Pat's past? It probably wouldn't be worth a story because nobody had ever heard of Pat Snell. But when Heather thought about how Pat had sat there as quiet as a mouse, listening in on her conversation with Cail, she decided to see what she could dig up anyway.

Pat glanced up. "What are you staring at?"

"Still trying to figure out where I've seen you before."

"You haven't."

"I think I have. I never forget a face, but sometimes

I have a hard time putting a name with it."

"I probably resemble somebody else you've met." Pat returned to her book for a moment, then glanced up. "Look, Heather, all I want from you is to be left alone. Every time I look up, you're watching me."

"I wonder why it upsets you so much," Heather mused.

"Just stop it!" Pat snarled and went back to her book.

But Pat's mind was far from the book. Of all the nerve! The woman had tried on her glasses! And now Heather knew that Pat didn't really need glasses. What would she make of that?

She had to figure out what to do about Heather Brackland. The woman was going to cause trouble for her; she could feel it. Ignoring Pat's request to be left alone, Heather continued to stare at her. Sooner or later, Heather would put the pieces together, and when she did . . .

Disaster.

Pat closed her eyes, imagining the story spread all over *The National Scoop*, and picked up by other newspapers and TV newscasters. They'd have a field day. Well, she couldn't let that happen. *Could not.* No way would she allow Heather Brackland to destroy the career she'd spent twenty years building. She took a deep breath, opened her eyes, and stared at her open book. The print swam before her eyes. It made her feel sick.

Heather continued to watch Pat, thinking. She could tell Pat was aware that she was looking at her, but the woman pretended to be lost in her book. Heather was developing a hearty dislike for this woman.

Pat had made such a fuss over the pictures that Heather was tempted to take some more shots of her, just for the hell of it. Pat still had her head buried in her book, her profile turned to Heather, who wondered if she could snap a couple of shots now without Pat's being aware of it.

Worth a try. A smile played with her lips as she let

her arm slide down to the side of her chair. Quietly, she felt around for her camera, but couldn't find it. It must be under the chair. Damn, she'd have to get up to retrieve it.

She stood and bent down to look under the chair. The camera wasn't there. She wheeled on Pat. "Where is it?"

Pat looked up, startled by Heather's outraged tone. "What are you talking about?"

"My camera! And don't look at me with those cow eyes. I know you took it! You were the only one here when I came in."

Pat closed her book and folded her arms across her chest. "I've only been here ten minutes."

"Plenty of time for you to steal my camera and hide it."

"Don't be ridiculous."

"You've been griping all day about how you don't want your picture taken. So you decided to do something about it. I'm warning you, Pat. You better hand it over right now."

"I didn't touch your camera," Pat said through gritted teeth.

"Liar!"

"Good grief, you are nuts. Anybody could have taken it before I got here."

Chapter 9

As Tess came in from outside, she heard Heather shout, "Tell me where it is, you bitch!"

Tess hurried into the parlor to find Heather advancing on Pat Snell, who sat in an armchair, leaning back to get away from Heather. Seeing Tess, Pat shoved Heather away and struggled to her feet. "This woman is crazy, Tess. Stay away from me, you idiot!"

"What's going on here?" Tess asked.

"She hid my camera!" Heather said.

"No, I didn't. I haven't even seen her camera since we came back from our run this morning."

Tess knew that was a lie, as she'd seen Pat looking at the camera just before she went upstairs to read the assigned chapters from Dr. Patrice's book. "Are you sure, Pat?"

"Of course I'm sure!"

Tess did not want to contradict her in front of Heather. Besides, she had only seen Pat looking at the camera. She hadn't seen her touch it. "It has to be around here somewhere."

At that moment, Lillith and Rudy entered the parlor. "Heather has misplaced her camera," Tess told them. "We were about to look for it."

"Good riddance," Rudy muttered, dropping onto a soft cushion with a grunt.

Tess, Heather, and Lillith searched the room.

55

Pat, who sat back down in her chair and opened her book, pretended indifference to the activity going on around her. But Tess suspected, from her high color and the tensed muscles in her jaw, that Pat was far from indifferent.

Finally, the only place left to look was under Pat's chair. "Would you mind getting up for a minute, Pat?" Lillith asked.

With a disgruntled sigh, Pat stood. Lillith dropped to her knees and thrust her arm under the chair. "I think I found it," she said and pulled the camera out. "Oh, dear . . ."

The film case was open and the film was gone. Worse than that, the camera was smashed, as if it had been hit with something heavy. Or stomped by a big foot, Tess thought, glancing at Rudy Hansel's wide, thick-soled athletic shoes.

Heather cried out and grabbed the camera from Lillith's hand. "It's destroyed! Pat did this!"

"I did not!" Pat protested.

"It was under your chair!"

"Do you think I'd be stupid enough to leave it under my chair if I'd done it?"

Heather clutched the ruined camera to her chest like a mother protecting her child from the neighborhood bully. She wheeled on Rudy, who was sprawled on the loveseat. He didn't manage to wipe the grin off his face before Heather saw it.

"It was you, then! I'll get you for this, Rudy Hansel!"

Rudy lumbered up out of the soft cushions with some difficulty, his face red. "Lady, you don't know who you're dealing with. I can ruin you."

"You should know about being ruined, right Rudy?"

He staggered back as if he'd been hit.

Watching him worriedly, Lillith inserted herself between the two. "How dare you accuse my husband without a shred of proof!"

"He *said* he'd smash my camera—in the support session. Everybody heard him!"

"That's not proof," Lillith said. "He was just sounding off."

"You want proof?" Heather spat the words. A drop of spittle glistened in the corner of her mouth. "I can get all kinds of proof! About many things!"

Lillith glanced at Tess with a puzzled look. Turning back to Heather, she said, "Cail was right. Nobody with any standards would work for your newspaper. You are truly an evil person."

"Oh, yeah? Well, you're no angel yourself, *Barbie*!" With that, Heather stormed toward the parlor door, where the other guests were gathering. She pushed past an open-mouthed Dorinda Fenster and ran up the stairs.

Marcia, who had been craning over her sister's shoulder, shook her head. "The atmosphere in this house is certainly not conducive to spiritual renewal. It's squeezing my soul."

Nobody bothered to respond to that.

Tess was still looking at Lillith, who'd turned as pale as a ghost.

"That proves it," Rudy said. "You all heard her call my wife by the wrong name. Heather Brackland is certifiable!"

Lida and Cail came into the parlor, having witnessed at least part of the scene just played out there.

"Does that woman make trouble wherever she goes?" Lida asked of no one in particular.

"I think you should ask her to leave, Lida," Cail said.

"I totally agree," Pat put in.

Lida was thoughtful. "I don't know. I'd have to give her back her registration fee."

"Rudy's right," Dorinda said. "She's nuts."

"She's just a little confused," Lillith said, her voice trembling.

Tess wondered why Lillith was defending Heather, particularly since she still looked as if she'd been punched in the stomach.

After lunch, as the guests retired for the afternoon break, Marcia found Tess in her apartment.

"I was looking around last evening and found your

tower room with all the books. Is it all right if I spend
my break up there?"

"Of course," Tess assured her. "Guests are welcome
to use the library anytime."

"Oh, good. I need to be alone. With all the bad vibes
floating around here, I need to get in touch with my
spirit. I have to reestablish my serenity."

Tess wondered exactly what that involved. A crystal
ball? A séance? With Marcia Yoder, anything was possible. She was tempted to ask, but didn't want to en-
courage Marcia to rave about her guru, as Tess had
heard her doing to Lillith earlier.

"Go up any time you feel the need," Tess offered.

During the afternoon break, Rudy and Lillith returned
to their suite. "Why don't you lie down?" Rudy suggested. "Maybe you can catch a nap." He was worried
about her. Since the discovery of Heather's smashed
camera, Lillith had been distracted, nervous almost. At
lunch, he'd noticed her lower lip trembling.

"I'll just sit on the couch," she said, waving a hand.

"You feeling OK?"

"I'm fine," she said sharply. Then, "I'm sorry, sweetie. I didn't mean to snap at you."

"It's that woman," Rudy snarled. "Not getting enough
to eat is bad enough without sharing meals with Heather
Brackland."

Lillith laid her head back on the sofa and gazed up at
him. "It's worse than living with a poisonous snake."

She sounded thoroughly depressed, and it wasn't like
her. He sat down beside her and took her hand.

"Rudy," she murmured, "can you imagine anything—
any circumstance—that would make you stop loving
me?"

What's going on here? he wondered. If anybody
should be secure in her marriage, it was his wife. He'd
loved his first wife, had found her comfortable to be
with. But Lillith—he literally worshipped the woman,
and sometimes that scared him. He still found it almost
impossible to believe that Lillith was his wife; he wor-

ried constantly that he might lose her. Not that she'd
ever given him cause to think that. It was just his own
insecurity rearing its ugly head. Down deep, he was sure
he didn't deserve Lillith.

"Never in a million years."

She turned her head toward him. He was amazed to
see tears shimmering in her eyes. "Promise?"

He reached out and pulled her into his arms. "I swear
it. I don't like the effect that woman is having on you—
on us. Maybe we should pack right now and get out of
here."

"No. I—I can't leave now."

He held her away from him to peer into her beautiful
face. "Why not? You can't be enjoying this."

"Rudy, I think we should talk to Heather. Maybe you
could offer her money."

"Not a dime! My God, Lillith, you don't pay off people like Heather Brackland."

She buried her face in his shoulder. "Rudy." Her voice
was muffled against his shirt. "If she finds out what I
did . . ."

"Oh, come on, it can't be that bad."

"I'm the one who destroyed her camera."

For a moment, he didn't know what to say. He'd have
guessed it was anybody else in the house before Lillith.
She hadn't been half as upset as he was when their wedding story appeared in *The National Scoop*. Maybe fear
of being found out was what was making her so nervous.
That had to be it, he thought, and felt a vast rush of
relief.

He laughed. "Is that the circumstance you're afraid
might make me stop loving you? Good God, sweetheart.
All I want to do is congratulate you. Good for you! You
were great when you were helping look for the camera.
You seemed so concerned. Never knew you could put
on such a false front."

She sat up to stare at him. "False front? What—what
do you mean?"

"I just told you—the way you acted when you were
looking for the camera."

She pressed her face against his shoulder again. "I hit it with a dumbbell. I did it for you, because you were so upset about her taking pictures of us." Then she got up and went to the bathroom. In a moment, she returned with a roll of film. "I didn't know what to do with this," she said.

Rudy took it, pulled the film strip all the way out, exposing every frame. "I'll get rid of it," he said. "And don't worry about it. Nobody will suspect you. Even if it comes out, we'll just pay for the camera."

His assurance should have allayed her anxiety, but it didn't seem to. "Maybe I will lie down for a few minutes," she said, sounding as if the weight of the world had settled on her shoulders.

In the Carnaby Room, Heather was typing an e-mail to *The Scoop*'s head researcher, requesting a background check on Pat Snell of Topeka, Kansas. Not that she expected anything interesting to turn up, but Pat's overreaction to having her picture taken continued to intrigue Heather. She had an instinct about these things, and right now her instinct was telling her that Pat was hiding something. Whether it would be worthy of publication in *The Scoop* was another question.

As she was about to log off, a voice said, "You've got mail." She clicked on the little mailbox at the bottom of her screen and saw she had an e-mail from the researcher. She double-clicked to bring the message up.

Proof arriving by priority mail. Still digging.

How enigmatic. She typed in a response—

Proof of what?

—then clicked on the "send" icon.
The reply came back within moments.

Wait and see. I promise it'll be worth it.

The researcher was playing games, making her wait to find out what the "proof" was. Well, it should be there later this week. She could wait and continue work on the Rudy story.

In the meantime, she had to get to town and buy another camera.

Chapter 10

"We decided on yellow roses and daisies," Tess said. She and Luke were enjoying thick steaks at a restaurant just down the street from Cinny's bookshop. "Does that sound OK to you?"

Luke's hand closed over hers on the red-and-white checked tablecloth and squeezed gently. "It sounds perfect."

She flashed a brief smile. "You don't really care, do you? Do you even know what daisies look like?"

He grinned airily. "Of course I do. They're those little white flowers, right?"

She nodded. "Aunt Dahlia insists on adding a few salmon-colored roses for the church and my bridal bouquet. She says they'll look good with my hair."

He ran an approving glance over her curling auburn hair and the top of her royal blue silk dress. "You will look great regardless. Anything you want is fine. All I want is you, my darling. Whatever it takes to accomplish that is OK by me."

Tess laughed. "Aunt Dahlia will be pleased. She was afraid you'd dislike what it took us three hours to settle on."

Blond brows arched sardonically over amused blue eyes. "Three hours? To decide on the flowers?"

"Well, that wasn't all there was to it. We had to meet with the caterer, too, and plan the menu. But I could have done the whole thing in an hour, without Aunt Dahlia. She wanted to go over every detail a million times. Oh, by the way, the centerpiece for the reception buffet will be a huge ice sculpture of a bride and groom. That was Dahlia's idea, and I just decided to grin and bear it. With Dad in Paris, Aunt Dahlia is the closest relative I have here. And she loves planning grand events."

Luke released her hand to cut a bite of steak. "She'll probably be even worse when Cinny and Cody Yount get married," he said, shaking his head. "Poor Cody."

His tone was just offhand enough to rouse her suspicion. She looked at him sharply. "Do you know something I don't?"

He laid down his knife and leaned comfortably on one elbow. The corner of his mouth twitched. "Maybe."

"What? Luke Fredrik, stop teasing and tell me!"

He ate a bite of steak before replying, while Tess fidgeted in her chair. Her cousin and the young attorney Cody Yount had been together for a year, much longer than Cinny had ever dated any man. But Tess had heard nothing about marriage.

"Cody told me the other day that he'd proposed," he replied, serious now, "but you can't tell anyone. Especially Dahlia."

Tess was delighted. "Wonderful. Have they set a date?"

"Whoa, sweetheart. Cinny promised to think it over. Do you suppose she's toying with Cody?"

"Of course she is. Cinny loves drama. She gets it from her mother. But she'll say yes. I'm sure of it. They'll probably wait until after our wedding to announce the engagement."

Luke, suddenly aware of the diners at a nearby table, sent a glance over them. No one seemed to be paying the least attention to their conversation. He lowered his voice. "Until they do, we can't breathe a word of this to anybody else. I swore to Cody. He knows when they make the announcement, Dahlia will take over." Luke made a clicking sound with his tongue. "Poor Cody," he said again.

For a moment, Tess felt a stab of regret. "Cinny's lucky to have her mother." Tess's own mother had died when she was a child. Her father had remarried and had two children, teenagers now, with his second wife. They lived in Paris, where her father was in the diplomatic corps.

Evidently Luke heard the wistful edge to her words, for he changed the subject abruptly. "Anything new at the retreat?"

"Actually, yes. Somebody destroyed Heather Brackland's camera. She accused two of the guests, both of whom denied knowing anything about it."

Luke gave her an arch look. "Which they would, if they were responsible."

Tess nodded. "One of the guests did it, that's for sure. But which one? Nobody seems to like Heather, so it could have been any of them."

"Didn't you say the Brackland woman had taken pictures of all of them? Must be somebody who didn't want his—or her—picture developed."

"If that's true, then it has to be one of the Hansels. They're the only ones at the retreat who are well-enough known for Heather to want to do a story about their weight-loss efforts. Except—" She paused thoughtfully. "Well, Pat Snell did make quite a point of not wanting her picture taken."

"If Heather no longer has a camera, things will probably calm down now."

Tess had too many questions about her guests to be sure about that. Cail and Heather still looked at each other as if they could kill, given the chance. Pat Snell couldn't stand Heather, and even Lida watched Heather like a hawk, especially when Cail was around. Of course she also watched Lillith, whom Cail found irresistibly attractive, a fact he didn't bother hiding. And Lida would be watching Marcia Yoder now, too, since Marcia had flirted outrageously with Cail at lunch.

"It'll be okay, honey," Luke assured her.

"I'm sure you're right." Tess wanted to convince herself, but she was not totally successful.

"And if I'm not, your guests' problems aren't yours. Let them deal with them."

They finished dinner and rose to leave. "Let's go back to my apartment and open a bottle of wine," she suggested.

"Lead the way."

It was raining the next morning when the guests came downstairs, where Lida and Cail waited for them in the foyer. Tess, who'd just left her apartment, had stopped to chat with the two and greeted the guests individually as they descended the stairs.

Heather wore a yellow raincoat with a hood; apparently she was the only one of them who'd thought to bring rain wear, though a couple of the other guests carried umbrellas. Cail had on water-repellent Gor-Tex pants and a T-shirt. Lida was the only one who wore shorts with her tank top. The others had on slacks or sweatpants.

"That rain isn't letting up," Rudy announced happily. "Guess we'll miss our morning constitutional."

"A little rain won't hurt you, Rudy," Lida said.

Lillith, who'd been staring at the back of Heather's yellow-swathed head—while Cail watched Lillith with hooded eyes—seemed to shake herself and turned to Rudy. "You can use my umbrella, sweetie. I don't mind getting wet."

"We can't go walking in the rain," Kent protested.

"Of course we can," Lida told him. "People do it all the time. You'll enjoy it."

Clearly, Kent would not enjoy it. "Do we have to, Dad?" he asked.

Lillith gave her husband a meaningful look, and his shoulders sagged. "If everybody else is going, I guess we'd better, son. We can look forward to a nice, hot shower when we get back."

"Come on, everybody," Cail said. "We'll do our stretches on the veranda." He looked back at Lillith.

"You want to help me lead the run this morning, Lillith?"

Rudy stiffened and Lillith said quickly and dismissively, "I'll walk with my husband."

Cail shrugged indifferently, but Tess had seen the flash of anger in his eyes before he turned away. Obviously Cail was not accustomed to getting the cold shoulder from women, married or not.

Forty-five minutes later they had returned to Iris House, all of them soaked to the skin except for Heather, who hung her raincoat in the guest closet off the foyer while the others went to put on dry clothes.

Heather came into the kitchen, where Nedra was finishing her raisin bran, Gertie was busy at the range, and Tess was sipping coffee from a big mug.

"What are you serving us this morning, Mrs. Bogart?" Heather asked.

"Breakfast burritos," Gertie told her.

Heather peered over her shoulder. "Smells good, but I can't believe you can fix burritos without oodles of calories in them."

"The tortillas are nonfat, and I'm using fat-free egg substitute and turkey bacon. They're not bad, actually. I tried one. I'm serving them with tangerine slices and salsa. I think you'll find them more substantial than the bran flakes you had yesterday morning."

Nedra snorted in disbelief and slowly savored a bite of cereal and half-and-half.

Heather wandered into the dining room where she helped herself to coffee from the urn.

Tess remained in the kitchen as the guests ate breakfast. She wanted to be on hand if tempers flared again. But everybody seemed relatively subdued.

"I need to pick up a few things in town," Heather announced. "Lida, can you give me a ride in your van?"

Lida gazed at the other woman, plainly wishing she would disappear. "I don't know when I'd have the time."

"How about during the morning break," Heather said, turning her gaze from Lida to Cail. "If you can't, maybe

Cail could accommodate me. You do want to accommodate me, don't you, Cail?"

Cail's expression tightened.

"I'll take you," Lida said quickly, and Tess wondered if she was afraid to let Cail and Heather out of her sight. There were rumors that Lida and Cail had a romantic as well as a professional relationship. Lida appeared to be insecure about the relationship, whatever it was, probably because of the age gap between her and Cail. But from what Tess had overheard, she didn't think Lida needed to worry about Heather. Marcia Yoder might be another matter, however. She had made it plain how much she would like to start a relationship of her own with Cail.

"There will be a full moon tonight," Marcia said suddenly. She was gazing adoringly at Cail. "I plan to celebrate by dancing in the moonlight at midnight."

Dorinda rolled her eyes helplessly. "It could still be raining at midnight," she said.

Marcia gave a lilting laugh. "So much the better. I love feeling the rain on my skin." She smiled coquettishly at Cail. "Every inch of my skin."

Good Lord, Tess thought. It sounded as if she planned to "celebrate" in the nude.

"Anybody care to join me?" Marcia asked, glancing around the table, then bringing her gaze back to Cail, who gave her a secret little smile before ducking his head.

Kent Hansel spoke up. "I might."

Rudy scowled at his son. "No, you won't, young man."

Kent looked down, embarrassed.

Nobody else offered to join Marcia. But as soon as Marcia and Dorinda left the dining room, Rudy said, "That Marcia's one strange lady. Is she actually going to go out tonight without a stitch on?"

"Sure sounded like it to me," Lida said.

"Well, I don't know about the rest of you," Heather said, "but I wouldn't miss Marcia's little celebration for the world." All eyes snapped on her. She looked around the table and laughed. "Only as an observer, of course."

It seemed to be Marcia's day for stirring things up. When it was time for the morning support session, Tess was in the kitchen, waiting while Gertie made out a grocery list—a few things Tess would pick up when she ran errands in town. She heard Lida ask what the group would like to discuss.

When nobody spoke up right away, Marcia chirped, "We could have an honesty session."

Dorinda said warningly, "Marcia . . ."

Marcia laughed, ignoring her sister. "Don't look at me like I've slipped a cog. We do this all the time in a group I belong to at home."

"I'm not sure what you mean," Lida ventured.

"We say truthful things about each other, maybe things we've been wanting to say for a long time. Like somebody once told me that I have pretty feet."

Tess heard Rudy's muffled laugh, and then Lillith shushed him.

"I see," Lida mused. "Each of us would tell what we admire about the others. All right. It could give us all a boost. Let's try it. Marcia, would you like to go first?"

"Sure. Pat, I've been wanting to tell you that I like your haircut." She patted her own locks which, like Pat's were clipped short and hugged her head.

Pat looked at her suspiciously. "Why . . . er, uh, thank you, Marcia."

"But I have to say also—because we must tell the whole truth—that you shouldn't dye your hair. Black is too stark a contrast with your skin. I would guess that your hair is naturally light brown, or even blond."

Dead silence followed Marcia's speech. Then Tess heard footsteps and peeked around the kitchen door frame. Pat, back stiff, was leaving the room. Heather, an inquisitive look on her face, watched her leave. Dorinda sat in an armchair with her head in her hands, clearly mortified by her sister.

"I thought we were going to say nice things about

each other," Lida said, her voice taut with irritability.

"It's an honesty session," Marcia protested. "I was only telling the truth. That dye job is really terrible. Somebody needed to tell her—for her own good."

Lida's mouth turned down at the corners. "Let's forget the honesty session and talk about aversion therapy."

"Aversion what?" asked Lillith.

"Pick something fattening that you love—like chocolate cake," Lida explained. "Then think of something else you hate—like castor oil. Then, every time you're tempted to eat chocolate cake, close your eyes and imagine it drenched in castor oil. Now, let's each tell the group what food we can't resist, even though we know it's bad for us."

Later in the morning, when Tess went out to check on the workmen, she almost ran into Kent and Donnie Armory, who stood at the side of the house, their heads together.

Tess heard Kent say, "I'm telling you the honest-to-gosh truth. We can see a naked lady."

Donnie giggled. "You're making that up."

"I swear—" Suddenly, Kent looked around and saw Tess. "Come on, Donnie," he said. "I still got twenty minutes of my break. Let's go up to my room and play cards or something. Oh, and bring those cookies your Mom sent. Stick 'em in your pocket so my stepmother won't see them."

Tess watched them run toward the front door and wondered if she should mention the conversation to Lillith or Rudy. She thought about it. No, Kent was just an adolescent boy trying to impress a peer. Rudy would never allow his son out of the suite at midnight.

Cail had opted out of dinner with Lida and the others, preferring to return to his apartment and stick something in the microwave because he couldn't stand another minute of Heather Brackland without losing what little patience he had and strangling her. Literally.

Pacing his apartment, he imagined his hands on Heather's neck, pictured her gasping for air, her face growing blotched and purple. Heather dead. What a relief that would be.

He truly believed he could murder her, if he thought he could get away with it. Hmmm, could he possibly? It would be tremendously risky. Maybe he could think of some other way to silence her. Paying her what she demanded would do it, but there would be no end to that, even if he had the initial three thousand plus. Eight hundred dollars a month for years would put a serious kink in his budget. The fact was, he had no intention of paying Heather a cent. Just thinking about it made him want to hit something with both fists.

On to Plan B. Could he terrorize her into keeping quiet? Heather was tough; she had to be to work for that tabloid. But she wasn't a fool, and she had a healthy sense of self-preservation. The question was, could he scare her badly enough to make her drop her demands?

He grabbed a Gor-Tex jacket and left the apartment, running through the rain to his car.

In the Darcy Flame Suite, Lillith was curled against Rudy's side on the loveseat in the bedroom. They were watching a late movie on television. Kent was asleep on the roll-out bed in the living area of the suite, exhausted from more exercise than he'd had in any forty-eight hour period in years.

Rain tap-tapped against the window panes. The weather had cleared in the afternoon, but about an hour ago, the rain had resumed.

"Looks like we might have to get soaked again on our walk in the morning," Rudy said, glancing dolefully toward a window.

"The rain will probably stop before then," Lillith said.

"Do you really think that squirrelly Marcia will go out in this without any clothes on?"

Lillith smiled. "I have no idea what Marcia will do. She's an odd woman. I think Dorinda is embarrassed by her."

"Don't blame her."

"I never saw two such different sisters in my life."

"What was all that stuff Marcia was telling you this afternoon?"

"Apparently she's involved in a group—a cult or something. She talked about a man named Ahmed and said he's the most honest and spiritual person she's ever known and she's trying to be like him. She said lies and secrets destroy the soul. The way she looked at me, Rudy . . ." She shuddered. "It was almost as if she could see into my mind, as if she knew everything about me. I felt very uncomfortable. I had a real strong feeling she was trying to convert me."

"She's insane."

Lillith muttered sleepily. "Well, she's different."

They watched the romantic comedy in silence for several minutes. Then Lillith said, "I don't think I'll be able to stay with you till the end. I'm going to bed."

Lillith didn't seem herself this evening. It worried

him. He picked up the remote and switched off the television set. "Let me check on Kent and I'll join you."

She kissed his cheek, murmured, "Good," went into the bathroom to change into her nightgown, then slipped into bed. A moment later, Rudy crawled in beside her.

She turned into his arms. "You don't think Kent will try to sneak out at midnight, do you?"

He nuzzled her cheek. "That kid dies when he hits the bed, and he's out like a light."

"Like father, like son," Lillith murmured.

"I love you," he whispered into her ear.

"No matter what?"

Lillith had never seemed unsure of herself—or him— before. What was going on with her?

His arms tightened around her. "No matter what."

The phone rang in the Carnaby Room. Heather, who was at her computer, considered letting it ring. But it might be Cail telling her he had the money. Stretching her arm out, she managed to snag the receiver without getting up.

"Hello?"

Silence. Her mind was still on her story, but as she refocused she could hear a distant tinkling sound, a singer who sounded like Willie Nelson and a raucous male laugh in the background. No one said anything into the receiver.

Heather waited. The caller breathed into the phone.

"Who is this?"

"Keep your mouth shut and get out of town," he said, "or you're gonna get your face rearranged." Then the line went dead.

A chill skipped up Heather's spine as she replaced the receiver. The voice had not sounded familiar.

In the Black Swan Room, Lida paced the carpet and checked her watch. A quarter till twelve. She stopped by the phone and dialed Cail's number. For the fifth time, there was no answer. Where *was* he?

She wandered to the window and peered out. The pale

light from a yard lamp was fuzzy in the rain. She couldn't see the backyard from her vantage point. Presumably, Marcia Yoder would be "celebrating" behind the house, where she couldn't be seen from the street. On the other hand, the woman didn't seem to care who saw her. She'd invited everybody in the house to join her. No one had taken her up on it, of course. Not in Lida's hearing, anyway. Although Heather had said she'd "observe" the celebration. Probably meant to take pictures if she could do that in the rain.

Heather might have thought she'd put one over on Lida when she taxied her to the drugstore that afternoon. She'd waited in the car for twenty minutes until Heather returned with her purchases—toiletries, she'd said. But Lida had seen a roll of film in Heather's sack. Either she had brought two cameras with her to Victoria Springs or she'd slipped out of the drugstore by way of the back alley and bought one in the camera shop next door.

She was going to have to deal with Heather—and soon. The woman was spoiling the retreat for the others.

Right now, though, her mind was on Cail, who wasn't at home, which meant he might be planning to meet Marcia at midnight. She'd certainly made it clear she'd love his company, and Lida had seen the devilish smile he'd given Marcia—the smile that made her go weak in the knees when Cail turned it on her.

Lida and Cail had been intimate several times in the past four months and, as far as Lida knew, he wasn't seeing anyone else on a regular basis. He'd even said he loved her, but the words had slipped so easily from his mouth that Lida suspected he had said them frequently, to other women. And she was sure he'd had a relationship with Heather Brackland before he came to Victoria Springs.

Even though he assured her he wasn't interested in Heather, she felt uneasy every time the two of them were out of her sight at the same time. Cail claimed Heather had started stalking him back in L.A., but Lida was beginning to wonder if that was the whole story. He'd

warned Lida several times not to believe anything
Heather said about him, so often in fact that she was
beginning to think he protested too much. And if
Heather was obsessed with Cail, it didn't appear to be
out of love. More like hate.

So why did she feel so uneasy about Heather? Lida
despised herself for being jealous when Cail was around
other women, which he was all the time at the fitness
center. But she couldn't help herself. The man she was
in love with attracted females like a magnet drew steel
shavings—and, what was worse, he didn't seem to dis-
courage the attention.

She tried Cail's number again and let it ring ten times,
then slammed down the receiver. Lately he'd called her
every night they weren't together, but it was already too
late to expect to hear from him tonight.

It didn't mean anything that he'd missed one night,
she told herself. He'd probably gone to that bar he fre-
quented. He knew she hated it when he went there because he always got drunk. But, for once, she wished
she could be sure he was at the Red Dog instead of with
Marcia Yoder.

She settled in a chair and tried to relax. Looking at
her surroundings, she realized that in spite of its masculine furnishings, she liked the Black Swan Room. The
massively scaled bed was lacquered in a reddish-brown
color, the same color as the bearded iris pictured in the
print on the wall above a cane side table. The huge bu-
reau and marble-topped washstand were lacquered with
the same dark hue. In contrast, two gooseneck reading
lamps attached to the wall above the bed sported fluted
white shades, and the ruffled side drapes on the windows
as well as the paneling above the wainscoting were white
too. Below the wainscoting, the walls had been papered
with a bold black-and-white print. An intricately pat-
terned rug covered most of the polished oak floor, its
black and gray tones relieved by bright splashes of
lemon yellow. There were other touches of yellow in
throw pillows, bed linens, and the comfortable wing-
backed chair where Lida sat.

Cail would look wonderful in this room. Her stomach muscles immediately tensed as Cail took over her thoughts once more. She got up and began pacing again. As attractive as the Black Swan Room was, she couldn't pace it all night without screaming.

Maybe she'd slip outside and see what she could see. But she'd better wait until a few minutes after midnight to give Marcia and Heather, and whoever else might have decided to join them, time to leave the house. She wouldn't want to run into anybody in the foyer.

Lida hated insecurity in other women, and even more in herself. If Cail was in attendance, she'd just as soon he didn't find out she was checking up on him.

Chapter 12

Tess hesitated just inside her apartment door. It was almost midnight. Unable to sleep, she'd gotten up and put on a sweatsuit and a raincoat. But now she wondered if she should get involved in whatever was happening outside. If anything *was* going on. It was still raining and, even though Marcia had said she would celebrate in the rain, Tess doubted it. For one thing, it must be less than fifty degrees out there and, with the rain, it would feel even cooler. Surely no one in her right mind would run around nude in such weather.

Ah, but there was the rub. Some of her guests doubted Marcia *was* in her right mind, and hadn't been shy about saying so. But, of course, Marcia wasn't actually insane, Tess told herself. Marcia simply marched to the beat of a different drummer.

Still, maybe she should have a look.

As Tess stepped into the foyer, she heard a door on the second floor open and a woman's voice, in a low but urgent tone, say, "Don't do this, Marcia." Dorinda Fenster.

Marcia said something that Tess couldn't understand—probably that she intended to go outside whether her sister approved or not. Then the door slammed and footsteps padded down the upstairs hall. Tess quickly stepped back into her apartment and eased the door quietly shut.

Marcia was barefoot and naked beneath her light robe, which she'd decided to wear until she actually started to dance. In fact . . . She hesitated in the foyer. An umbrella would be nice, too—only until she was ready to begin. She could dispense with the umbrella when she disrobed, which she envisioned herself doing slowly, peeling off her robe like a striptease dancer, when Cail arrived—if he arrived. But the way he'd smiled at her when she'd announced her plans for tonight made her believe he'd be there. Cail struck her as a guy who was always on the prowl. But she wasn't looking for a long-term relationship, just a little fun.

After she was naked, she'd watch him disrobe. Imagining his muscular body moving in the moonlight made a shiver of expectation skitter up her spine.

Too bad she was sharing a room with her uptight sister; otherwise, she'd take Cail back upstairs with her. Maybe he'd invite her to his place.

Remembering the coat closet beneath the stairs, she opened the door to look for an umbrella. No umbrella, but a couple of sweaters and a yellow raincoat hung on the rod. The raincoat looked like the one Heather Brackland had worn that morning. Well, Heather wouldn't be needing it tonight. Marcia took the raincoat from the hanger and slipped it on, pulling the hood up over her head as she slid back the dead bolt, opened the front door, and stepped out on the veranda.

A loud clap of thunder woke Rudy Hansel from a sound sleep. He leaned up on an elbow to peer at the illuminated dial of his watch. Two minutes till midnight. A perfect night to be snug in bed with his wife. He lay back down and reached for Lillith.

His arm closed on nothing. He sat up and switched on a bedside lamp. The sheet on Lillith's side of the bed was thrown back, and she was gone. Must be in the bathroom.

He switched off the light and reclined, waiting a few moments. When she didn't come back to bed, it occurred to him that she might be ill. She hadn't been herself this evening.

Worried now, he again switched on the lamp and padded to the bathroom, tapping softly on the closed door. When there was no response, he opened the door. The bathroom was unoccupied.

If she was restless, she may have moved to the couch to keep from disturbing him. He went around the Chinese screen to the living area of the suite. Lillith wasn't on the couch or anywhere else in the room. And his son's bed was empty, too.

How many times had he imagined such a scene? He, awaking or coming home after work, to find that Lillith had gone, left him with nothing but a note saying the marriage had been a mistake and she wanted a divorce. But he saw no note, and besides, if she ever decided to leave him, she wouldn't take Kent with her.

He felt a stab of panic. Where in hell were they?

Fighting growing uneasiness, Rudy pulled on a pair of slacks and a shirt, slipped into his shoes, and left the suite. By then, it was five minutes past midnight.

Tess was about to leave her apartment for the second time that night, when she heard footsteps descending the stairs. Was everybody in Iris House stirring tonight? She heard whoever had come downstairs open the front door and go outside.

Primrose, reclining in her favorite chair, peered at Tess as though asking where she thought she was going at that ungodly hour. Tess leaned back against the door, chuckling to herself. Evidently she wasn't the only one who was curious about Marcia's "celebration." Even before she heard the person she assumed was Marcia come down, before she'd given up trying to sleep and gotten out of bed, she'd heard what sounded like stealthy footsteps in the upstairs hall.

There wasn't much sleeping being done around Iris House tonight, that was certain.

Maybe she should simply go back to bed and leave them all to get drenched, wandering around in the rain like a bunch of escapees from a loony bin. As Luke had pointed out on more than one occasion, she was merely the innkeeper, not her guests' mother.

She took off her raincoat and tossed it on the couch. Primrose lifted her head and stretched. Still not sleepy, Tess went to the kitchen to brew a cup of herbal tea, with Primrose following on her heels, hoping for a treat.

Kent Hansel crouched behind a bush in a corner of the backyard where he'd promised to meet Donnie. They'd chosen the place because they could reach it without being seen from the backyard, yet it provided a good view.

But where was Donnie?

Maybe Donnie's dad had caught him trying to sneak out. Would Donnie say he was supposed to meet Kent? The little twerp better not rat him out.

But the longer Kent stayed there, the more chance of his father or Lillith waking to find him gone. He'd give Donnie another couple of minutes before he gave up and went back to bed. At least here, burrowed in under the leafy shrub, he wasn't totally soaked yet.

Nothing much to see in the backyard, anyway. Somebody was wandering around in a raincoat. In the dim light from the yard lamps, it looked yellow. Must be Heather Brackland. She acted like she was waiting for somebody.

Then he saw another figure on the far side of the yard. It was too dark to tell if it was a man or a woman. The figure halted when he saw the person in the raincoat and slowly backed up, farther into the shadows. Now Kent couldn't tell if the other watcher was gone or hiding in the dark.

Crouching down like this made his already sore thighs ache. He raised up a little and the tip of a branch scratched his cheek.

"Ouch!" He slapped one hand over his mouth and used the other to push the branch away.

The person in the raincoat stopped walking and turned toward Kent's hiding place. "Who's there?"

His heart thundering in his ears, Kent froze.

"Cail, if that's you, don't be bashful. Come on out."

Good grief, please don't let her catch him!

After a few moments, the person in the raincoat turned away and began pacing again. Kent realized he'd been holding his breath and let it out slowly.

Man, that was close, and the longer he stayed there, the bigger the chance of somebody seeing him. There would be heck to pay if he got caught out here.

It was starting to look like weird Marcia wasn't coming after all, and he was beginning to get really wet. He straightened and peered over the bush. Still nobody but the person in the raincoat was in sight. But he sensed other eyes watching.

He shivered, wishing he had a raincoat too, or at least a jacket, but he'd been too afraid of waking his dad or Lillith to grab more than the clothes he'd dropped by the bed, before leaving the suite.

He began to shake. With cold, he told himself, but down deep, he knew that part of it was fear. Every shadow had started to look like a human shape. Although he wouldn't admit it to a soul, it was scary out here in the dark. Was it really worth getting wet and cold just to see weird Marcia naked?

If he didn't go back inside soon, he'd get caught for sure. His dad slept like a log, but he wasn't certain about Lillith. Anyway, if Donnie was coming, he should have been here by now.

Quietly, he backed away from the bush and crept toward the front of the house.

Tess had finished her tea and, still not sleepy, she switched on the TV. An old Gary Cooper movie was showing. She got a quilt and curled up on the sofa. Primrose jumped up to snuggle with Tess.

Within ten minutes Tess's eyelids were drooping. She threw back the quilt, picked Primrose's limp form off her leg, switched off the television, and stumbled drowsily toward her bed.

She'd reached the kitchen when she heard a high, shrill voice from the foyer.

"Somebody help!"

Retracing her steps, Tess flipped on the foyer light, opened her door and peered out. Donnie Armory, his teeth chattering, stood in the foyer, dripping water on the stone floor. He wheeled toward the sound of Tess's door opening. His face beneath the freckles was milk pale.

She could think of only one reason for Donnie to be standing in her foyer, after midnight, soaking wet. Apparently she should have reported the conversation between the two boys that she'd heard that afternoon. But it hadn't occurred to her that they might actually manage to sneak out.

There was time for reprimands later, and there would be plenty of those for Donnie from Wayne. "Donnie?"

"Oh, Miss Darcy! There's somebody laying out in the backyard!"

"Who?"

"I couldn't tell. It's too dark. I think it's a woman. I tried to help her up, but she won't move."

"I'll get my raincoat," Tess said.

She brought a flashlight and a towel for Donnie, who was shaking so hard he could barely manage to dry his face and arms. "Let me get you a jacket."

"No!" He dropped the towel to the stone floor. "You have to come and help her. She was just walking around and then she acted like she heard something—and she walked into the dark and I didn't see her for a minute, and then she fell and I saw her legs sticking out of the dark and—she won't get up!" He was shaking harder than ever and Tess worried that he might be going into shock.

"I'll go, but you stay here." She ushered him into her apartment. Primrose looked up at the stranger on her turf, said, "Yoo-wl," and streaked toward Tess's bedroom.

"Call your father to come get you, Donnie," Tess said, "then wrap up in that quilt and wait for him here."

"It's only a block. I can walk."

"No," Tess said firmly. "Call your father."

"Dad's gonna kill me for slipping out."

"He may have already discovered you're gone. Your parents will be worried sick. Call them right now. You can use that phone there on the secretary."

As Tess returned to the foyer, Lida appeared on the stairs. "What's going on? I thought I heard somebody screaming." She was dressed in jeans and a denim jacket.

Tess didn't have time to explain about Donnie—who he was and how he happened to be there. "Evidently we have somebody lying in the backyard, hurt or drunk or something. I'm going out to see what's wrong."

"I'll go with you."

Flipping on the flashlight, Tess and Lida hurried through the house to the back door. Lida, she noticed, was leaving damp footprints on the carpet, but Tess would wonder about that later.

Just as they reached the back door, Tess thought she heard the front door opening. Somebody coming in? Or going out? Another thing to wonder about later.

They walked out into the backyard, where the rain had dwindled to a fine mist. Tess swung the flashlight beam around the yard until it fell on a figure, swathed in a yellow raincoat, lying near a back corner of the yard.

Lida drew in a deep breath. "That looks like Heather."

Of course. Tess remembered now that she'd seen Heather wearing the yellow raincoat that morning.

Tess started toward the figure and heard a rustling to her left. Rudy stepped out of the shadows.

"What are you doing here?" Tess asked.

"I—I just got here. I'm looking for Lillith and Kent. Have you seen them?"

"They're not in the suite?"

"Not when I left." He peered toward the huddled form. "What's going on?"

"Heather must have fallen or something," Lida said.

Tess hurried toward the fallen woman, who she noticed now wore no shoes. Lida and Rudy followed her cautiously. "Here." Tess handed the flashlight to Rudy, then knelt beside the figure on the grass.

"Heather?"

There was no response. Tess lifted the woman's head and pushed back the yellow hood. The flashlight beam illuminated her face.

"My God! It's not Heather!" Lida gasped.

Rudy remained silent, his hand shaking a little, causing the flashlight beam to waver.

Tess pressed a finger against the woman's throat, searching for a pulse. There was none. And when she gently laid the woman's head down, her hand came away wet with something that wasn't water.

"It's Marcia Yoder," she said, trying to see Rudy's face in the darkness, but it was only a blur. "Rudy, have you seen anyone else outside?"

"No. I told you, I just got here."

Tess scanned the dark perimeter of the yard. Whoever had killed Marcia could still be hiding there, she realized, and a spider of anxiety crawled up the back of her neck. There was a gate in the back fence and a narrow gap in the hedge. The killer could easily have escaped by that way. Even if it was somebody staying in Iris House, he or she could have gone out the back gate, circled around the yard, and entered the house via the front door. The sound of that door closing, as she and Lida had walked through the house to the back door, seemed suddenly ominous. Had it been the murderer?

The rain had stopped. Tess became aware that Lida and Rudy were watching her, as if waiting for instructions. "Rudy," she said, "would you stay here while I call the police?"

"The police!" Lida cried.

Tess held her hand out so that the flashlight beam fell on the blood covering her fingers and palm. Rudy and Lida stared at Tess's hand as if mesmerized.

Lida gasped. "That's blood!"

"Yes," Tess agreed. "Marcia is beyond our help.

Rudy, don't touch her and don't let anybody else come near her until the police arrive."

"Okay, but I still don't know where Lillith and Kent are. Oh, my God . . . if there's a killer running around loose—Tess, will you check the suite again?"

"As soon as I call the police. If I don't come back right away, that means they're safely indoors." Mentally Tess ran through what else should be done. "Lida, somebody should tell Dorinda. Can you do that?"

Lida gulped. "I—I guess so."

The two women walked back to the house.

Chapter 13

Tess's call was answered by an officer whom she hadn't met before, Ryan Struthers. He said he'd be there in ten minutes. As Tess hung up, Wayne Armory arrived to pick up Donnie.

"You've got a lot to answer for, young man!" Wayne greeted his son, who stood before him, head hanging in humiliation. "I would never have believed you'd do this, Donnie. I'm sorely disappointed in you."

"It's the first time I ever slipped out, Dad. Honest. And I sure wish I hadn't. I—I found a lady in the backyard. She's hurt bad." Tess hadn't had the heart to tell him that Marcia was dead.

Wayne turned a befuddled look on Tess. "What lady?"

"One of my guests," Tess said. "Marcia Yoder."

"What were you doing in Tess's backyard, Donnie?" Wayne demanded.

"I was supposed to meet Kent—you know, the boy who's staying here. He said a naked lady would be dancing out there at midnight. But I never saw a naked lady. And Kent didn't come."

"He was probably pulling your leg, son." Wayne glanced at Tess. "Where's this Yoder woman now, Tess?" Wayne asked. "Can I help?"

"There's nothing you can do, Wayne. It's best if you just take Donnie on home."

Wayne grabbed his son's arm and ushered him out the door, threatening dire punishment. As soon as they left, Tess ran upstairs to the suite. Lillith answered her knock. She wore slacks and a long-sleeved shirt, and her hair, hanging loose about her shoulders, was wet. It was awfully late for her to have washed her hair, so Tess guessed Lillith had been outside, too.

"Is Kent with you?" Tess asked.

Lillith nodded. "He's in bed."

"Rudy's looking for you both. He says he woke up and you were gone."

"I—I went in search of Kent. He just admitted to me that he wanted to see Marcia do her thing. I guess she didn't come because he gave up and came back inside right after I left. We just missed each other. Then I got back here and Rudy was gone."

Tess studied the ex-model's beautiful face. Was it the face of a murderer?

Marcia had been wearing Heather's raincoat, and the two women were about the same height. With the hood pulled up, Marcia could easily have been mistaken for Heather. Tess couldn't forget how Lillith's face had drained of color when they'd found the ruined camera and Heather had lashed out at the Hansels, insinuating that she had scandalous information about the couple. And she'd called Heather *Barbie*. Rudy had attempted to pass it off as the babbling of a crazy woman, but Heather wasn't crazy. Vindictive, maybe, but not crazy.

Who was Barbie? Tess filed the question away to come back to later.

Pushing her suspicions about the Hansels aside for the moment, she told Lillith what had happened. Lillith's mouth made a perfect O. She looked genuinely shocked, but then models had to be good actresses, didn't they?

"You'd better get Kent up and dressed again," Tess said. "The police will want to talk to everyone."

As she left the suite, Lida came out of the Arctic Fancy Room. "How's Dorinda?" Tess asked.

Lida shook her head, her hand still on the half-open door. "Not good. She's blaming herself for letting Marcia leave the suite, even though she begged her to stay. I tried to tell her she couldn't have stopped Marcia, but she said she should have gone with her."

"The police will be here any minute. They'll want to talk to everyone. Would you ask Dorinda if she feels up to coming down to the parlor?"

Tess made one more stop at the Carnaby Room. Heather, fully dressed, came to the door. "Have you been outside tonight?" Tess asked.

Heather went immediately on the defensive. "Why?" She was used to asking questions, not answering them.

"You said you were going to observe Marcia's celebration," Tess reminded her, sounding more accusatory than she'd intended.

Heather cocked her head. "I would have, too, but I couldn't find my raincoat. I thought I put it in the foyer closet, but it's not there and—"

A siren sounded in the distance. "That will be the police," Tess said.

"Police!"

"I haven't time to explain right now. I'm asking everybody to gather in the parlor downstairs."

"But, what—"

Tess waved the question aside. "It will all be explained in a few minutes." She went to meet the police.

Officer Ryan Struthers was a stout young man of medium height, with white-blond hair and a birthmark the size of a dime on his left cheek. He'd brought Chief of Police Desmond Butts with him. Butts, still puffy-eyed from sleep, was in his usual disgruntled mood.

"So," Butts said, "what kind of mess have you got yourself into this time, Tess?"

She had learned to ignore Butts's sarcasm. "Come and see." She led them to the backyard. Rudy was standing where she'd left him, still holding the flashlight beam on Marcia, staring as if he couldn't look away. He was shivering now from the cold.

Butts bent over and felt for a pulse. Straightening, he barked, "Anybody touch her?"

"I did," Tess admitted. "I lifted her head up, to make

sure she wasn't breathing. There's a lot of blood on the back of her head."

"What was she doing out here in the middle of the night?" Butts asked irritably.

"She said she was going to dance in the rain," Tess told him. "In the nude."

Butts's mouth dropped open. "Say what?"

"That's what she said," Tess went on.

"She isn't naked."

"I guess she never got around to that," Tess said.

"Marcia Yoder was crazy as a loon," Rudy put in.

Butts wheeled on him. "And who are you?"

Rudy stiffened. "Rudy Hansel, president of Hansel Enterprises. I'm a guest here."

"You were out here, too?"

"Not till—later," Rudy stammered. "After Tess and Lida found her."

Tess glanced at him, wondering how truthful he was being. He had come out of the shadows—he could have been there for some time.

Butts glanced at Tess. "This Lida he mentioned, would that be Lida Darnell?"

Tess nodded. "She's staying here—conducting a weight-loss retreat."

"Sounds like half the town was out here in your yard," Butts grumbled. "Struthers!"

"Yes, sir."

"Go back to the car and call an ambulance. Then secure the crime scene. Tess, I want to look around here a few minutes, then I need to talk to everybody who's staying here."

"I thought you would," Tess told him. "I've asked them to gather in the parlor."

Butts ran a hand across his bristly burr cut. "You got the routine down pat, don't you, Tess? Getting to be an old hand at murder."

"Through no fault of my own," Tess told him.

They were all there, waiting, when Chief Butts came inside, even Dorinda, who wore an old-fashioned floor-length, faded rose chenille robe over her nightgown. Her eyes were red and she kept dabbing at them with a handkerchief. Everybody else had on street clothes.

First, Butts took down everyone's name and home address, asked what each one did for a living, and made his usual speech about not leaving town without his permission. As in previous instances, Tess was amazed that nobody challenged him. Most people just assumed Butts had the right to make such demands, when in truth he could do nothing to stop them from leaving, short of arresting them. As an attorney, Dorinda would know that, but she was probably too dazed to contradict the police chief.

Butts began questioning them, one by one. Nobody but Dorinda admitted to knowing when Marcia left the house. "It was close to midnight," Dorinda said, her soft voice wavering, "maybe a few minutes before. I didn't look at the clock."

"Can you explain to me what your sister meant to do in the backyard at midnight?"

"Communing with the night, she called it," Dorinda told him. "She was involved with this group—New Age, I guess you'd say. For one thing, they advocate doing away with clothes."

Butts looked at her for a moment, then shook his head in disbelief. "She was a nudist."

"Sort of—I mean, she didn't go to nudist camps. She felt that was hiding. She would have gone naked everywhere, all the time, if she hadn't been afraid of being arrested. I know it sounds bizarre," Dorinda said. "I thought so, too. I tried to talk sense to my sister, but she wouldn't listen."

"Actually," Tess said, "I heard Marcia leaving the house and Dorinda begging her not to go."

Dorinda blinked and looked at Tess. "You were still up?"

"I think the whole house was up," Tess said. "I heard several people coming and going around midnight."

"I only came to the retreat to keep an eye on Marcia," Dorinda murmured. "She has always had whims, and she would act on them without thinking. I thought I could protect her. I—I should have been with her." She pressed the tissue to her eyes again.

Butts took charge. "Okay, I want to know who left this house tonight, what time, where they went, and how long they were gone."

Rudy and Lillith spoke up first. Lillith went in search of Kent, and Rudy went in search of Lillith and Kent. With Butts standing over him, Kent had to admit that he'd slipped out to see a naked lady, waited for Donnie Armory to show up, finally got tired of waiting when neither event materialized, and returned to the house.

Butts made a note to speak to Donnie Armory, then scanned the faces of the others. "Who else went outside tonight?"

"I went out with Tess," Lida said, "after I heard Donnie calling for help. He'd found Marcia lying in the backyard."

She'd been out before that, Tess thought, remembering the wet footprints Lida had made on the carpet. She started to mention it, then decided she'd ask Lida about it later.

Kent's head came up. "Donnie was here? I never saw him."

"He must have gotten here after you were back in the house," Tess said.

"Somebody came up behind Marcia Yoder and hit her hard enough to kill her," Butts said. "We found a dumbbell against the back fence, in a flower bed—small, like maybe it was used as a hand weight. It could be the murder weapon. Anybody have any idea where it might have come from?"

Several people started to talk at once. Butts held up his hand. "One at a time!"

"I brought several dumbbells from the fitness center for the retreat," Lida said. "They're over there in the corner." She went to the pile of dumbbells, looked through them, and straightened up with an expression of horror on her face. "One of the five-pound ones is missing."

"We'll have the dumbbell examined, then store it in the evidence locker," Butts said. "Now, it sounds like most of you went outside sometime tonight. Didn't anybody see or hear anything unusual?"

Nobody spoke for a long moment. Lida glanced at Pat Snell, as if expecting her to speak. When she didn't, Lida said, "Pat's room is next to mine. I—I thought I heard her leaving her room a few minutes before I heard Donnie calling for help."

All heads swiveled toward Pat, who glared at Lida through her eyeglasses. "I—I came down to the kitchen to get something to eat." She lifted her chin defiantly. "I found some ice cream in the freezer and took it out. I'm sorry, Lida, but I couldn't sleep because I was so hungry. I tried that aversion therapy thing, but it didn't work. I finally managed to overcome the temptation before I dipped any ice cream from the carton and went back to my room—still hungry."

Lida shook her head. "Tomato juice was available."

Butts's bushy brows rose, as if wondering if Lida really thought tomato juice was a substitute for ice cream. "Miz Snell, did you hear anything from the backyard while you were in the kitchen?"

"No. I was only in the kitchen a couple minutes."

"Anybody else see anything?"

"I saw the lady in the raincoat," Kent said. "She was just walking around the yard—like she was waiting for somebody. But then I came back inside."

"What about you, Mrs. Hansel?"

"I didn't see anybody. I guess I didn't go far enough to see Marcia's body. I just made sure Kent wasn't in the yard, called his name a couple of times, and came back to the house."

"So." Butts gazed around the room, his spectacle lenses spotted with a few dots of rain, his blunt features sagging with fatigue. "Sometime between the time the victim left her room and Donnie Armory arrived, one of you killed Marcia Yoder."

"One of *us*?" shrilled Pat Snell, her hand flying to her mouth.

"If that dumbbell turns out to be the murder weapon," Butts said, "it had to be one of you."

"Before I came in," Kent said suddenly, "I thought I saw somebody in the shadows, watching the lady in the raincoat."

Butts spun to face him. "Could you tell who it was?"

"No, sir."

"Was it a man or a woman?"

Kent lifted his shoulders. "I couldn't tell, sir. It was just a shadow."

"None of this makes much sense, people," Butts said. "If this broad—excuse me Miz Fenster—if Marcia Yoder was going to get naked, why did she bother wearing a raincoat?"

There was a long silence. Finally, Heather said, "I didn't even know Marcia brought a raincoat with her. She didn't have it on when we went for our run this morning—or I guess it was yesterday morning now."

Rudy looked at Lida, who looked at Tess. "She was wearing your raincoat, Heather," Tess said. "She must have taken it from the foyer closet."

Now everybody was looking at Heather, whose expression was one of slow comprehension as understanding dawned. "*My* raincoat?" Understanding was followed by trepidation, and then panic. She shot to her feet and cried, "They thought it was me! Somebody wants to murder me, Chief Butts."

"Oh, really?" Butts asked wearily. "Why is that?"

Heather looked around the room. "They all hate me."

"How long have you known these people?"

"Only two days, but—"

"I hardly think they could have come to hate you enough to want to kill you in two days!"

"They do, though!" Heather insisted. "And I had a phone call this evening. The caller didn't identify himself, but he told me to keep my mouth shut and leave town or I'd get my face rearranged."

Butts looked skeptical. "Man or woman?"

"It was a man. I didn't recognize the voice."

Butts peered at Rudy Hansel, and pointed a finger. "You're sure it wasn't him?"

Rudy stiffened and began to bluster. Butts quieted him with a hard look.

Heather shook her head. "I don't think so."

"It must have been somebody here," Butts told her. "He's the only man I see."

"It—it could have been Cail."

"That's the biggest load of bull I ever heard," Lida blurted, her eyes flashing at Heather.

Butts glanced at Tess. "Who's Cail?"

"She means Cail Marrs," Lida said. "He works for me, but I'm positive he wouldn't kill anybody."

"You don't know him as well as you think you do, Lida," Heather told her.

Lida glared at her. "Why are you so intent on causing trouble for him?"

Butts inserted a question. "Did he have a key to the house?"

"Not unless one of the guests gave them theirs," Tess said.

Nobody admitted to doing that. "Then how did he get his hands on the dumbbell?"

"Cail is here during the day. He could easily have taken it earlier," Heather said. "We only use them for a half-hour a day. Nobody would have noticed if one of them was gone, at least not until tomorrow—today rather—when we're supposed to use them again."

Lida gave her another poisonous look.

"Where is this Cail?" Butts asked.

Lida hugged herself, her head lowered. Finally, she said, "He has an apartment at the fitness center."

Butts made another note on his pad. "I'll talk to him."

"Chief Butts," Heather wailed, "I won't be safe until you arrest the killer."

"Which I would gladly do," Butts snarled, "if you could give me one iota of evidence against anybody. So far all I'm hearing are wild accusations."

"If you don't take me seriously, I'm going to end up dead—like Marcia," Heather insisted.

"I will investigate your accusations against this Cail," Butts told her, "but I can't arrest a man without solid evidence."

"I'm sure *he* was responsible for that threatening phone call I got earlier," Heather said.

"Why?"

Heather twisted her hands together. "I know he wants me to leave town. I—I remind him of things he'd like to forget. We knew each other in L.A., you know, before Cail moved here."

Butts looked more interested now. "That's fascinating, but you said you didn't recognize the voice."

Heather opened her mouth to speak, then shut it again.

"Like I said," Butts snapped, "give me some evidence against *somebody*, and I'll take it from there."

Chapter 14

Under Butts's skeptical scrutiny, Heather perused the faces turned toward her. She hesitated on Pat's face, and then Rudy's. Finally she dropped her gaze. "I don't know who's trying to kill me," she admitted finally. "But somebody destroyed my valuable camera. I need it in my work. If you can discover who did that, you'll have your murderer."

Tess saw that Lillith's complexion had suddenly turned ashen, but nobody else seemed to notice, except Rudy, who took his wife's hand in both of his, as if to comfort her.

"I don't understand why somebody would destroy your camera," Butts said.

"They didn't want their picture taken," Heather explained.

Butts snorted. "I've heard of camera shy, but that's kind of extreme, isn't it?"

"Of course it is," Heather agreed. "This is an extreme person we're dealing with."

"Damaging a camera," Butts told Heather sternly, "is a far cry from murder."

"I tell you the murderer is in this room," Heather insisted, "or it's Cail. He hates me more than anybody."

"Young woman," Butts said, "are you on medication?"

"No!"

"Well, maybe you should be," Butts said. "You seem to be suffering from paranoia."

"Why won't anyone believe me?" Heather broke into sobs and ran from the room.

Butts took off his glasses and used a handkerchief to polish the lenses. Sighing heavily, he put them back on. "OK, that's all I need you people for right now. You can go to bed, but keep yourselves available for further questioning. Oh, Miz Fenster, I need a word with you before you go."

Mutely, the other guests trailed out and up the stairs. Butts waited several moments, then said to Dorinda, "Are you up to coming to the hospital morgue in the morning? Tess already ID'd the victim, but she's only known her a couple of days. We need somebody close to the victim to make an official identification."

Dorinda blanched, but she nodded. "I—I guess so."

"I'll go with you, Dorinda," Tess said.

"Would you, Tess? Thank you." Dorinda rubbed her hands together agitatedly. "I keep hoping I'll wake up and find this has all been a bad dream." She glanced at Butts. "I'll need to make arrangements to have the body sent home."

"There will be an autopsy, ma'am," Butts said. "It's routine in cases like this. I'll let you know when you can claim the body."

Dorinda nodded, her throat working to swallow tears. When she didn't move to leave, Butts said gruffly, "You can go now." Dorinda left the parlor, her head down.

Butts glanced at Tess. "Communing with the night," he mumbled. "Where do you find these people, Tess?"

Tess lifted both hands. "They find me."

"What's the story with that Heather Brackland?"

"She works for a national tabloid newspaper. She was taking everyone's picture, supposedly for before and after shots, so they could see how much they'd improved in two weeks. But when they found out who she worked for, several of the guests asked to have their pictures and the negatives. Rudy Hansel was the most vocal. I gather

Heather did an unauthorized story about his recent wedding."

"Is he somebody important?"

"He's a wealthy real estate tycoon, and his wife is—or was—an internationally known supermodel. I guess that makes them tabloid-worthy."

"Hummph. Anybody else here who's famous?"

"Not to my knowledge." Tess pondered a moment. "There is one other thing I should tell you, though. I overheard Cail Marrs and Heather Brackland having a heated conversation. She told you that they knew each other in Los Angeles—that's where Heather lives—before Cail moved here. I think they were romantically involved. She said he owed her money, and he made veiled threats."

"Hmmm, I'd better check on this Cail first thing tomorrow."

"Oh, and at one point, Heather called him Cail Hurst. I don't know if Hurst or Marrs is his real name."

Butts made another note. "I'll check both names. Sure sounds like Heather Brackland has made plenty of enemies, and the murdered woman *was* wearing her raincoat."

"Yes, and Heather told everyone that she was going out to watch Marcia's celebration, so they all expected her to be there."

"Still, we need to check out Marcia Yoder, too. Had she had any problems with any of the other guests?"

"Not that I know of. Nobody was quite sure how to take her. The first day she suggested that she'd like to exercise in the nude, but Lida quashed that idea immediately. She was different, but there didn't seem to be any harm in her. I can't imagine why anybody would want to kill her."

Butts thought about that for a minute. "Anything else you want to tell me?"

Again, Tess recalled Lida's wet footprints and, again, she decided to keep her own counsel for the time being. "Nothing I can think of right now. I'll let you know if something occurs to me later."

"You do that," Butts grunted as he stuffed his tablet into his shirt pocket and clomped out of the parlor. At the front door, he turned back to say, "If any of these people decides to check out of Iris House, let me know immediately." Then he was gone.

Tess got a mop and cleaned up several spots of mud which Butts had tracked into the foyer.

She thought about going up to Lida's room right then and asking her why she'd lied to the police, but decided that tomorrow would be soon enough. She was asleep on her feet, and in a very few hours it would be time to get up again.

Before she could get into bed, her telephone rang. With a weary sigh, she lifted the receiver. "Yes?"

"Tess, this is Pat Snell."

"Yes, Pat."

"I overheard something." She spoke in a low conspiratorial tone. "It was during our morning break. I was alone in the parlor, going over the reading assignment, and I heard Heather and Cail talking in the foyer. Do you think I should tell the police or what?"

"I heard them arguing before that," Tess said. "It sounded as if Cail and Heather cosigned a mortgage in L.A., and he skipped out on her. She wanted him to pay his share. I've already told the police about that."

"What I heard sounded like blackmail."

"Really?"

"Heather said if Cail didn't pay her, she'd tell the Los Angeles police where to find him."

"Oh, dear. I certainly think the police should know that. Do you want to call Chief Butts tomorrow?"

"I'd rather you did it, if you don't mind."

"All right."

"Good night, Tess."

With a reflective frown Tess hung up. Pat didn't want to get involved with the police, but she had certainly seemed to relish telling Tess what she'd overheard.

Blackmail?

Tess wondered if Heather was blackmailing anybody besides Cail. Whether she was or not, she had quickly made enemies of most of the other guests with her picture-taking and veiled threats.

It now appeared that one of them had decided to shut her up, and had mistaken Marcia for Heather. Nobody but the Hansels would seem to be of enough public interest to warrant tabloid coverage. Would Rudy or Lillith kill to keep their names out of *The National Scoop*? What could Heather know that was embarrassing enough, perhaps even sinister enough, to put her life in danger? Or was it Cail, after all?

Would the murderer try again?

Cail did not appear the next morning. Lida led the morning run alone, saying that the trainer was not feeling well and they would go on as before—keeping busy would take their minds off the horrible tragedy that had occurred last night.

Dorinda remained closeted in her room. When the other guests were at breakfast and it seemed clear that Dorinda was not coming down, Tess brought her a tray.

Dark smudges under Dorinda's eyes bore witness to a night of little sleep. She still wore the chenille robe, as if she had not taken it off since Butts had questioned the guests in the parlor.

"I brought you some toast and tea," Tess said. "You need to eat something."

Dorinda shook her head. "I'm not sure I can."

"Please try."

Dorinda sighed and stepped back so that Tess could enter. Two suitcases lay open on the unmade bed, and clothes were strewn about.

Tess set the tray on a side table. "Are you leaving?"

"Oh, no, I can't go until I can take Marcia with me." She glanced at a pile of clothes on a chair. "I—I was packing Marcia's things." She looked around helplessly. "I haven't found her journal, though. I thought she told me she brought it with her—it would mean so much to me to have my sister's journal, Tess." Her voice wobbled and she looked suddenly, desperately alone and vulnerable. "I must have misunderstood her. I'll probably find it in her apartment back home."

Tess put an arm around her shoulders and led her to a chair. "I'm sure it will turn up. Now, sit down and drink a cup of tea at least. You are going to need your strength." Tess poured from the china teapot and placed the cup in Dorinda's hands.

Dorinda sank back in the chair and took a sip. "This is good," she murmured.

"Maybe you could get down a piece of toast, too," Tess prompted gently. "Chief Butts called earlier. He wants us to meet him at the hospital at ten."

She set the cup down and buried her face in her hands. "I'm not sure I can go through with that, Tess."

"Just one glance at her face is all it will take, and I'll be with you."

After a moment, she dropped her hands. "All right. I know it has to be done."

"Yes. I wish somebody else could do it, but you're the only one here who really knew Marcia."

Dorinda blinked back tears. "Odd you should say that, Tess. Just yesterday Marcia said I'd never understood her, and I fear she was right." She shook her head sadly. "The things she would do continually surprised me. Our minds certainly didn't operate the same way. She was more like a daughter to me than a sister, you know. I took care of her from the age of twelve until she married. I was only twenty-two myself when our parents were killed."

"That's a heavy responsibility for a twenty-two-year-old," Tess said.

Dorinda nodded. "But I wanted to keep her with me. She'd already lost her parents in the car wreck, and we had no other close relatives. I couldn't abandon her to strangers. So, I took her with me to Austin to the university where I was enrolled in law school."

"How in the world did you manage that? I've heard law school is very demanding. How did you hold down a job and keep up with your studies and supervise Marcia?"

"Fortunately, I didn't have to work. The driver of the truck that hit our car was at fault. I was driving, and for a long time I asked myself if there was anything I could have done to have prevented the crash. But it happened so fast . . . he ran a red light. I knew enough, even at that young age, to get a good attorney, and the settlement was enough to see Marcia and me through the three years in Austin and the next couple of years while I got established with the corporation in Denver, where I still work. I'm head of the legal department now."

"Well, at least something good came out of losing your parents."

"I've tried to look at it that way," Dorinda murmured. She glanced at the toast on the tray, grimaced, and looked away.

"Would you like me to stay with you a while longer?" Tess asked.

"Thank you, but no. I'll be all right."

"Then I'll meet you in the foyer at a quarter to ten."

"Yes—yes, I'll be there."

Tess left her staring into space, her breakfast growing cold on the tray.

A short while later, as the other guests left the dining room for the morning support meeting, Tess asked to have a word with Lida in her apartment. Cail had still not arrived, and Lida told her charges to wait for her in the parlor and discuss aversion therapy until she returned.

When the two women were seated on Tess's sofa, Tess said, "You lied to the police last night, Lida. I haven't mentioned it to Chief Butts. I wanted to talk to you first."

Nervously, Lida plucked at the hem of her shorts and wouldn't look at Tess. "I don't know what you're talking about," she said, with much less indignation than there should have been if she hadn't lied.

"You told Chief Butts that you hadn't gone outside last night until you went out with me when we found Marcia's body. But your shoes were wet. You left damp footprints on the carpet as we walked through the parlor."

Agitatedly, she rolled up the hem of her shorts, then smoothed it out again. When she finally met Tess's gaze, her face crumpled. She looks old, Tess thought, realizing for the first time that Lida was probably in her forties. She kept her body firm and fit and knew how to use makeup to good effect, but the lines on either side of her mouth and at the outer corners of her eyes—which seemed more pronounced today than before—could not be camouflaged.

"I didn't want Cail to find out," she said jerkily, close to tears now.

"Find out what?"

Lida lifted her thin shoulders and took a deep breath. "That I was checking up on him. I—I kept calling his apartment last night, and he didn't answer."

Tess felt sorry for her. A woman in her forties with a twenty-something lover had good reason to feel insecure. "And you assumed he'd come to see Marcia?"

She cleared her throat and swallowed hard. "She invited him especially, and he didn't turn her down. I wanted to know if he came here, that's all."

"So you went out earlier. Was Cail here?"

She gave a hard shake of her head. "He wasn't, Tess. I swear."

"What time did you go outside—the first time?"

"Maybe five or six minutes after midnight. I saw Marcia walking about in that raincoat, but at the time I thought it was Heather. I only walked around the house far enough to see all of the backyard, and Marcia never knew I was there. I'd tied a scarf over my head and had on a jacket, but it was raining and I was cold. When I realized Cail wasn't here, I came back inside and tried his number again. He still didn't answer."

"And you didn't see anybody else outside?"

She gnawed on a red thumbnail for a moment. "No, but it was dark at the edges of the yard. Somebody could have been there and I wouldn't have seen him—or her."

"Yet you were sure Cail wasn't hiding in the shadows?"

Her eyes widened, but she shook her head. Still, Tess had seen the doubt in her expression.

"Then where do you think Cail was when you were trying to reach him?"

"Oh, he was tired—he skipped dinner because he said he needed to get some sleep. He was probably in his apartment all the time and had turned the phone off."

Tess didn't think Lida believed that for a minute. She sounded very much as if she were trying to convince herself more than Tess. "Does he make a habit of turning off the phone?"

Lida studied Tess's face for a long moment. "He could have been at the Red Dog." At Tess's questioning look, she added, "It's a bar west of town." Her hands suddenly folded into fists. "I hate it when he goes there. It's a sleazy place, with a low-class clientele." Tess wondered if she realized she was putting Cail into the same category. "The women—they wear too much makeup and their clothes are cheap and tight—they hang all over him." Younger women, Tess guessed. And she suspected they wouldn't come on to Cail if he didn't invite it.

"Have you heard from Cail this morning?"

"Yes. He called to say he wasn't feeling well and thought he'd stay in bed another couple of hours." She rolled the hem of her shorts up again. "Are you going to tell Chief Butts I lied?"

Tess pondered the question. "Not immediately. I'll think it over."

She let out a deep breath. "Thank you, Tess. Now, I really need to get back to the support session."

Chapter 15

When Tess and Dorinda returned from the hospital, Dorinda decided to go for a walk on her own. Anything to keep from staying in her room with Marcia's packed suitcases, Tess guessed. Viewing Marcia's still, white face had been difficult for Dorinda, but she'd managed to keep her composure long enough to make a positive identification. Butts had told them it would be a couple of days before the medical examiner could do the autopsy.

Cail had arrived while they were at the hospital and was leading the aerobics session when they got back to Iris House. Tess looked in on the group as they gamely tried to follow Cail's movements.

He looked dreadful. His eyes were red and puffy, and his face had a gray tinge. He looked, in fact, like a man with a serious hangover.

Tess went to her apartment and called Luke. She wanted him to hear about the murder from her, not the town grapevine. Then she reported Pat Snell's claim that Heather was blackmailing Cail to Officer Struthers, who happened to answer the phone at the station.

Struthers even volunteered something, which Butts would not have done. "This is good, Tess. That Hansel guy called a few minutes ago. He said his kid remembered that when he was hiding behind a bush in the backyard, he made a noise and the woman in the raincoat—Marcia Yoder, as we now know—called out Cail's name, and said he should come out of hiding. So she was expecting him."

"And if he came," Tess mused, "he'd have seen the yellow raincoat and assumed it was Heather."

After the aerobics session, there was a knock on her door. When she opened it, Heather stood there, shifting nervously from one foot to the other. She held Dr. Patrice Singleton's book with both arms against her chest, like a shield. "Can I come in for a few minutes, Tess? I'm too fidgety to sit in my room alone. And I know I can't keep my mind on the reading assignment."

"Sure. Would you like something to drink? Tea? Coffee?"

"Tea would be wonderful," Heather said as she sank down on the sofa, while Primrose vacated the sitting room, disappearing being her usual reaction to strangers.

Tess prepared two glasses of tea and handed one to Heather, who gulped the iced drink greedily. "I may actually learn to like this without sugar," she said with a slight grimace, and took another swallow. "My mouth is so dry. I guess fear does that to you."

"So you're still convinced the murderer was after you?"

She drained the tea from her glass, then curled her hands around it as if trying to absorb the coolness through her fingers. "Of course. Aren't you?"

"I have to admit it looks that way. And you *have* upset a number of people since your arrival here."

"Last night, I almost packed up and left. But Chief Butts said we shouldn't go without his permission and, besides, I decided I'd be better off here as long as I make sure there are people around me whenever I'm not locked in my room."

"Have you thought any more about who might have made that threatening phone call last night?"

She frowned. "Yes, and I'm sure it was a voice I'd never heard before."

"What exactly did he say?"

"At first he didn't say anything, but I could hear him

breathing. When I asked who it was, he said I should keep my mouth shut and leave town or I'd get my face rearranged. Just like I told the police. Then he hung up." She took a quick breath. "I did hear something else— before he spoke. There were noises in the background, music—a jukebox, I think, and what sounded like Willie Nelson singing."

"Anything else?"

"A man laughing, and something that tinkled—like wind chimes."

"Could it have been water running or ice being dropped into a glass?"

"It could have been. I was working at my computer and it was a moment before I really paid much attention."

"Hmmm." Tess was remembering Cail's late arrival that morning, and the signs that he was still recovering from a hangover. Apparently, he *had* been at the Red Dog last night—with women hanging all over him, no doubt.

After Heather left, Tess drove to the Queen Street Book Shop. Cinny's new assistant, a plump, middle-aged woman named Marge, had started work on Monday. If she worked out, she'd stay through the end of the November. Cinny handled the shop herself during the off-season months, when business was slow.

Marge was shelving new books when Tess entered the shop. She stopped what she was doing to greet Tess. "May I help you?"

"No, thanks. I'm Cinny's cousin, Tess Darcy. Is she around?"

"Oh, yes, Miss Darcy. Cinny has spoken of you often. She's working in the back room."

Tess found her cousin boxing books for return to the wholesaler. "I should have known I couldn't sell this ultra New Age stuff in Victoria Springs," Cinny said as she grabbed the packing tape dispenser and raked it across the top of the box, sealing the flaps. "I let the sales rep talk me into ordering it against my better judgment. He said these titles fly out of bookstores in California. I guess I forgot where I lived for a minute."

"He was handsome and charming, no doubt," Tess teased.

Cinny made a face. "Actually, he was fat and at least fifty, but quite a talker. He kept telling me how pretty I was. The oldest ploy in the book, and I fell for it." She looked embarrassed by the admission, but Cinny was pretty, with her long blond hair and bright blue eyes. With both hands, she raked her hair behind her ears and studied Tess. "I heard one of your guests died on you."

"Word does get around, doesn't it?"

"The rumor is it was murder."

"Looks that way," Tess admitted.

Cinny gave a sympathetic shake of her head. "I'm sorry, Tess." She tapped a bright red fingernail on the box she'd just sealed. "I glanced through one of these books. It was about a haunted house in Maine. They finally had to get a psychic to exorcise the ghost."

"Are you suggesting that Iris House has a ghost?"

Cinny shrugged. "I wouldn't go that far. But you do seem to have more than your share of trouble there. What could it hurt to call in a psychic?"

Tess laughed. "You can't be serious."

Cinny wrinkled her nose. "Only half." She glanced at her watch. "I could take an early lunch, if you're interested."

Tess was thoughtful. "Do they serve sandwiches at the Red Dog?"

Cinny's blond brows arched. "I don't know, but I don't think I'd want to eat anything in that joint."

Tess was surprised that Cinny knew of the place, since she herself had never heard of it until Lida mentioned it that morning. "Have you been there?"

"Of course not, but Cody defended a client who got into a brawl there. The owner brought suit against Cody's client and another guy for causing three thousand dollars' worth of damage. Cody's client claimed he was only defending himself, the other guy started it." She grinned. "Of course, all of Cody's clients are innocent victims of circumstance, to hear them tell it."

"Did Cody get him off?"

She shook her head. "The judge ruled in favor of the bar owner. He actually said that the defendant wouldn't have gone there unless he was looking for trouble. Evidently brawls break out frequently."

"Surely not this early in the day." Tess explained to her cousin that she wanted to find out if Cail Marrs was in the Red Dog the previous night at the time that Marcia Yoder was murdered.

Cinny's mouth dropped. "Cail Marrs! He's a cocky jerk, but you surely can't suspect him of murdering one of your guests."

Tess explained the mistaken identity theory and the fact that Cail owed Heather Brackland money and she had been blackmailing him for it. "Heather says she didn't recognize the man who made the threatening phone call, but Cail could have disguised his voice, then had a few beers too many and decided to kill Heather, anyway."

"How intriguing," Cinny said. "I thought that Cail Marrs was a sinister character the first time I saw him. He came in here, pretending to be looking for a book, and asked me out!"

"When was this?"

"About three weeks ago."

So, Lida had good reason to distrust her young lover.

"Well, I can't let you go to that place alone," Cinny stated. "It's not safe."

Tess couldn't suppress a smile. "I appreciate your concern," she said wryly. Cinny was always eager to get involved in Tess's little investigations, and Tess would have had to tie her up to keep Cinny from accompanying her to the Red Dog.

"Let me get my purse." Cinny said. "We can stop for a burger at Harry's Grill when we get back to town."

Chapter 16

Eighth Street took them through town where it curved into the state highway, which dipped and rose over hilly contours that, a little farther along, turned into the Ozark Mountains. The foothills surrounding Victoria Springs were green with trees lush with new leaves, and blue blankets of wildflowers covered the ground along the fencerows.

It was beautiful country, especially in spring, and Tess hoped to spend the rest of her days here.

The Red Dog, a couple miles out of town, sat like a lump of sludge on an otherwise pretty and peaceful landscape, surrounded by sparsely graveled dirt which was strewn with abandoned beer cans.

Inside, it was a big, barnlike saloon with a pool table and jukebox at one end, the bar at the other, and narrow, high-backed booths lining the remaining two walls. There were no windows, and the light bulbs in the few lamps hanging from the ceiling couldn't have contained more than twenty-five watts; consequently, even at midday, the interior was dim. The better to hide the dirt and grime that Tess could feel sticking to her shoes as she and Cinny entered.

The room was empty, except for a middle-aged couple in one of the booths, and at the end of the bar a bleary-eyed man in clothes that looked as if he'd worn them a week. He was already in his cups at noon.

The bartender, a burly man with a two-day beard and an anchor with a snake curled around it tattooed on his arm, stood under one of the dim lamps with his back to the cash register, a newspaper open on the bar in front of him and a stubby pencil in his right hand. He was attempting to work the crossword puzzle. Either he'd just started, or he wasn't very good at it, for he'd penciled in only a few letters.

He put the pencil down as Tess and Cinny approached, his face registering puzzlement.

"You ladies lost?"

Tess slid onto a stool and smiled. Watching her, Cinny followed suit. "I'd like a Coke," Tess said.

He looked at her without expression for a moment, then slid his gaze to Cinny, who had folded her hands in her lap to avoid touching anything. "Do you have Perrier?" Cinny asked.

The bartender grinned. "No, ma'am. We don't get many calls for it."

The drunk at the other end of the bar giggled, and tipped his shot glass to his mouth. He slid the glass down the bar, "Hit me again, Dudley."

Dudley ignored him, keeping his amused gaze on Cinny, who said, "Then I'll have a Coke, too. In the can, please."

Dudley grinned again, as though the idea that he might serve it any other way amused him. He reached down and pulled two Cokes from the refrigerator case below the bar, and set them in front of Tess and Cinny. "That'll be two bucks."

Tess laid the bills on the bar.

"Hey, Dudley!" the drunk called. "Keep your pants zipped and pour me a drink."

Frowning, Dudley walked slowly to the other end of the bar, stepped around it, and put a big hand on the drunk's shoulder. "Keep that dirty talk to yourself, Simon. We got some ladies present. And you can have another drink when you pay your tab."

"Aw, you know I'm good for it," Simon whined.

Dudley gripped Simon's skinny arm and pulled him off the stool. "Why don't you go somewhere and take a nap, Simon. You've had enough." With Simon protesting loudly all the way, Dudley dragged him to the door. The drunk stood there, leaning against the wall, as Dudley returned to his post behind the bar.

"Sorry about that." He looked from Tess to Cinny. "We don't usually get ladies of your—uh, caliber here. I know you didn't come in here for a Coke, so why don't you tell me what you really want."

Tess flipped the tab on her drink and took a sip. Before she had a chance to respond to Dudley, Cinny peered flirtatiously from behind a strand of blond hair. "We're looking for Cail Marrs."

Dudley laughed raucously. "You and about a dozen other babes."

The drunk snickered, and Dudley looked over at him. "Out, Simon. Now!" Simon slunk outside and Dudley looked back at Tess and Cinny.

"We need to see Cail on a business matter," Tess said.

He raked her with a dubious look. "What kind of business?"

"It's rather personal. You see, we had a meeting scheduled with Cail last night, but he never showed up. We thought perhaps you'd seen him."

He shook his head sadly. "Don't tell me you loaned him money, 'cause if you did you're not likely to get it back."

"Well—" Tess said, letting him draw his own conclusions. "We'd really appreciate any help you could give us."

He picked up a wet cloth, walked to the other end of the bar, removed the shot glass, and wiped away the ring it had left. "I ain't seen him today."

Cinny took a swallow of her Coke. "What about last night?" she asked, fingering the strand of pearls at her neck.

He tossed the cloth into a sink and propped his thick, hairy arms on the bar in front of Cinny and Tess. "Look,

I ain't information central. Why should I answer your questions?"

"We had hoped to handle this ourselves," Tess said, "and keep the police out of it."

He frowned. "I can do without the cops. Cail was here last night. He's here lots of nights."

"What time?" Tess asked.

He shrugged. "He came in late—about ten-thirty, I guess. Played a few games of pool, had a few drinks, and left."

"Did you notice what time he left?" Tess pressed.

"Look, lady, I don't keep tabs on my customers. I didn't notice what time he left. He was probably here an hour or so, but I wasn't watching the clock."

Which made it before midnight when Cail left the Red Dog. But he hadn't gone straight home, for Lida had called him a few minutes after midnight. It must have been about twelve-thirty when Donnie Armory found Marcia Yoder's body. Plenty of time for Cail to have left the bar, driven to Iris House, killed the woman he thought was Heather Brackland, and left before Donnie arrived for his rendezvous with Kent—and found Marcia Yoder's body instead.

"Did he use the telephone while he was here?" Tess asked.

The question seemed to require deep thought. Dudley frowned, worked his jaw, and finally said, "The phone's back by the pool table. Some of the guys who come in here use it to conduct business, like this is their office or something."

Tess suspected that the type of business the Red Dog's customers conducted did not require an office. "Is Cail one of them?"

He shrugged again. "Naw, he comes in to shoot pool and drink. He might make a quick phone call, setting up a date—that's about it."

"So you don't know if he used the phone last night."

"Nope. He could have, but like I said, I didn't notice."

Tess laid her hand on Cinny's arm and slid off her

stool. Neither of them had drunk half their Cokes. "Thank you for your time," she said.

As they walked to the door, Dudley called after them, "You ladies come back later. This place will be jumpin' by ten."

The drunk Dudley had thrown out of the bar was leaning against the trunk of Tess's car when they left the Red Dog.

"Let me guess," Cinny muttered. "He wants a lift."

"In his dreams," Tess whispered.

The drunk straightened up and gave them an ingratiating, slack-mouthed grin as they approached.

Cinny circled the front of the car and slipped into the passenger seat as soon as Tess released the door locks. "Would you please step back?" Tess said to the drunk as she opened the driver's door while trying not to breathe in his sour odor.

"I heard you asking about Cail Marrs," he said.

Tess hesitated beside the car. "Do you know Cail?"

He nodded eagerly. "See him a lot, here at the Red Dog. I can tell you where he lives."

"I know where he lives," Tess told him. "The bartender told me Cail was here last night. Did you see him then?"

"Yes, ma'am. Tried to borrow a fiver off him."

"Did you happen to notice if Cail used the telephone in the bar last night?"

His expression became crafty. "Maybe I did and maybe I didn't. Five bucks might help me remember."

Tess studied him for a long moment. He was probably conning her, but she took a five from her purse, tossed the purse into the back seat of the car, and wadded the bill in her hand. "If you saw Cail use the phone, that's worth five dollars to me."

He glanced at the hand which enclosed the five and licked his lips. "He didn't use the phone, but he paid another guy twenty bucks to make a call for him."

"What other guy?"

He shrugged. "Name's Chuck or Buck—something like that. He plays pool here once or twice a week."

"Did you hear what he said on the phone?"

"No, ma'am. But it wasn't much. A few words and he hung up. Then he gave Cail a thumbs-up sign."

Tess handed him the five and got into the car as the drunk shambled back into the Red Dog.

"He says Cail Marrs paid another man to make a phone call from the bar last night," Tess told Cinny as she drove out of the parking lot.

"I saw you give him money," Cinny said. "You sure he wasn't just making it up?"

Tess thought about it and finally said, "I think he was telling the truth. It fits the threatening phone call Heather Brackland got last night. She heard a jukebox in the background before the caller made the threat and hung up."

"Who made the call?"

"He claimed he just knew him by Chuck or Buck, didn't know the last name. He said Chuck—or Buck—plays pool at the Red Dog on a regular basis. I'll pass the information along to Chief Butts."

Cinny giggled. "I'm sure the chief will appreciate your helping him do his job."

"It could be important. I have to tell him."

"I know," Cinny said, wrinkling her elegant nose. "I'm kind of relieved you don't want to go back to the Red Dog to talk to the guy yourself."

"Once was enough," Tess assured her. "By the way, we won't mention our visit to the bar to Luke or Cody."

"I hear you," Cinny agreed. "Now, I want to wash the stink of that place off my hands and then get one of Harry's juicy hamburgers."

Later that afternoon, Tess stood in the kitchen, staring out the back window at the place where they'd found Marcia Yoder's body.

Gertie was checking the pantry to make sure she had everything she needed for the next day's breakfast and lunch. After a few moments she came back into the kitchen. "I'm going home now, Tess, unless you'd like me to keep you company for a while."

Tess turned from the window. "You go on, Gertie. I'll be fine."

Gertie shook her head sadly. "I swear, I don't know who would kill that poor, strange woman."

"The police think it could have been a case of mistaken identity. Marcia was wearing Heather Brackland's raincoat."

Gertie frowned fiercely. "Now that one I can see somebody wanting to kill."

The sun was out again and the temperature hovered at seventy, but it seemed chilly in the kitchen. Tess folded her arms, rubbing her upper arms with her hands. "Heather is convinced her life is still in danger."

A whoosh of air escaped Gertie's mouth. "Do you think so?"

Tess hugged herself. "Honestly, the killer would have to be incredibly desperate to try again. It's far too risky."

Gertie thought about it, and finally said, "Well, I'm going home now. You get back in your apartment and lock the doors."

Tess smiled. "Nobody wants to kill me, Gertie."

"Better to be safe than sorry," Gertie said ominously as she got her purse from the closet in the utility room and left by the back door.

Tess started back to her apartment just as Nedra came downstairs with her bucket of cleaning supplies. "Found this," Nedra said, holding out a yellow film canister with a string of film dangling from it.

Tess took the film. "Where was it?"

Nedra shrugged. "Wastebasket in the suite. Heard that Brackland say somebody stole her film."

"Thanks, Nedra. I'll take care of this."

"I'm off, then."

"See you tomorrow, Nedra."

Tess took the film to her office and dropped it into a desk drawer. Sitting at the desk, she looked out the bay window at the concrete foundation footings the construction crew had poured that day.

When Wayne and Donnie had arrived that morning, she'd gone out to tell Wayne that the woman Donnie had found in the backyard was dead and that he should expect Chief Butts to want to question Donnie. He'd said he'd break the news to his son, who appeared quite subdued by his midnight adventure. "Ask him if he remembers anything else from last night—anything he might have seen or heard," Tess had added, and Wayne had promised he would.

The men were gone now, to the lumberyard to order a load of lumber to be delivered the next day.

Tess sat at her desk for long minutes, thinking about the roll of film Nedra had found in the Hansels's suite. As far as Tess knew, they hadn't brought a camera with them to Iris House; she certainly hadn't seen them with one. Even if they'd brought a camera and taken a roll of film, they wouldn't have pulled it out of the canister like that, destroying the snapshots.

It would seem that one of the Hansels had, at the very least, removed that film from Heather's camera. Perhaps they'd destroyed the camera, as well.

Find the person who destroyed her camera, Heather had told Chief Butts, *and you'll have the murderer*, at which point Lillith had turned pale. Still, Tess wasn't as willing as Heather to make the leap from camera-destroyer to murderer, but the film was incriminating. She could take it to Chief Butts and tell him where Nedra had found it. Or she could confront the Hansels herself first and report to Butts later.

Chapter 17

"So here's where you found her," Luke mused. He and Tess had shared Chinese take-out in Tess's apartment, and now they were standing in the back-yard of Iris House, next to the large rectangle the police had outlined with yellow crime tape.

Tess bent over the tape to peer more closely at a spot on the grass. "You can still see some of the blood." Shivering a little, she moved closer to Luke. "I hate seeing this tape every time I look out a back window."

He put his arm around her. "The police will probably let you remove it soon."

"Butts came by today and walked around out here, but I forgot to ask him if I could take down the tape." Actually, Tess hadn't wanted to talk to Butts just yet, for she knew when she did, she should turn the film canister over to him. She wanted to talk to the Hansels first, but she hadn't found the opportunity before Lida took the guests out for dinner in her van.

"Let's get out of here," Luke suggested, "and go look at the new addition."

They walked to the side of the house. Luke wandered around inside the footings, pointing out where the new living and dining rooms would be. "Here's the new kitchen," he added. Then he

117

walked toward the back corner of Tess's current quarters. "And here's the master suite."

"It all looks smaller than the size the blueprints call for," Tess said.

Luke counted off the length of the addition by taking long strides of about three feet each. "No, they've got it right. All construction looks smaller than it is at this stage. You'll see when the walls go up."

"I can't wait."

Luke walked back to her and wrapped her in his arms. "Hey, you're shivering. Let's go inside."

In Tess's sitting room, Luke insisted that Tess sit down on the sofa while he got an afghan to cover her legs. "How about some hot chocolate?"

She rested her head on the back of the couch. "Sounds heavenly."

While Luke rummaged in her cabinets and refrigerator, then made the chocolate, Tess snuggled down in a corner of the sofa and closed her eyes. But behind her eyelids she could still see the yellow police tape strung around Marcia Yoder's body.

A few minutes later, Luke returned with two steaming mugs on a tray. "Here you go." He set the tray on the coffee table and settled beside Tess. She spread the afghan over both their legs and picked up her mug.

Studying her absorbed expression, Luke said, "You look tired, sweetheart. Maybe you'd better get to bed early."

"Too much on my mind to fall asleep," Tess told him. "Nedra found something today." She went on to tell him about the exposed roll of film the housekeeper had found in the Hansels's wastebasket.

"You're going to turn it over to Chief Butts, aren't you?"

She nodded. "As soon as I talk to the Hansels. I feel I should forewarn them." She blew on her hot chocolate before tasting it. "I'll speak to them when the group returns from dinner."

Luke was frowning. "If that film belonged to Heather Brackland, they're probably the ones who destroyed her camera. And if they're worried enough over what Heather might write about them to destroy the camera, then—" He trailed off thoughtfully.

"Then they might have been worried enough to try to kill Heather," Tess finished for him. "At least, that's what Heather will think. And the Hansels know that—they heard Heather tell Chief Butts that whoever destroyed her camera is the person who murdered Marcia Yoder. Which is why I want to confront the Hansels about the film. I want to see their reaction."

"I'd like to see that myself. We'll talk to them together."

Tess looked up at him in surprise. His customary reaction to her getting involved in a police investigation was to caution her to keep out of it. "Good. As soon as they get back, we'll go up to the suite."

"No," Luke said, "we'll ask them to come down here. Making them come to us might give us a slight edge."

Tess kissed his chin. "Good thinking, darling."

He turned her face to his and kissed her properly. Moments later, he said, "You could have a murderer living here, honey. The sooner he's rooted out, the better I'll feel about your staying here. And speaking of that, why don't you spend the nights at my place until this is all cleared up."

Wrapping her arms around his neck, she pressed her cheek against his. "You're as bad as Gertie. Nobody wants to kill *me*, love."

"Not yet, anyway," he muttered grimly.

Tess pulled back to stare at him blankly.

"If we start poking around, asking questions, who knows what the murderer will do? So. If Mohammad won't come to the mountain . . ." He paused to brush a kiss across her lips.

She pressed her face into the hollow of his neck, inhaling the masculine scent of him. "What does that mean?"

"If you won't stay at my place, then I'll spend the night here."

Tess snuggled closer and sighed contentedly. "Wonderful idea," she said serenely, "but not because I fear for my life. I just love having you around."

"Ah, my sweet Tess . . ."

Just as they were settling into another long kiss, the entrance door into the Iris House foyer was flung open so hard the doorknob banged against the wall. Tess and Luke sat bolt upright on the sofa.

Rudy Hansel's gruff, carrying voice rolled through Tess's apartment door. "Well, this has been a helluvan evening. I'm really sick of your accusations, Heather! We all are. You've probably got indigestion from that stuffed pepper you ate."

"He's right." That was Cail's deep voice. "You know I warned you when you ordered. You never were able to eat green peppers, Heather."

"You!" shrieked Heather. "You—you criminal! Keep away from me or I'll kill you!"

"Now, listen here." Cail's voice sounded menacing now.

"Heather," Lida said soothingly, "I have some antacid tablets in my room. You go lie down and I'll bring you a couple."

"I wouldn't swallow anything any of you gave me! Don't touch me!" Heather shrieked. "Get away from me, all of you!"

Tess and Luke jumped up off the sofa, and Luke jerked open the sitting room door. "What's going on out here?"

Pat Snell pointed a finger at Heather. "This crazy woman is at it again. All we heard all the way home is that we're trying to poison her. According to her, it's a group effort now, a big conspiracy."

Dorinda Fenster, whom Lida had had to coax to go to dinner with the group, covered her face with her hands. "I can't stand this right now. I really can't."

"Heather—" Tess said.

Lillith suddenly jumped away from Heather. "Oh, my God—"

Tess was already halfway across the foyer when Heather gagged, clutched at her mouth, and began to vomit on the flagstone floor.

Chapter 18

Tess, Luke, and Lida sat in the emergency waiting room, watching the curtained cubicle where the attendant had taken Heather and waiting for the doctor to emerge.

"On the drive home from the restaurant in my van," Lida said, "Heather kept complaining that something was wrong with the food she ate, that she felt sick. I'm ashamed to say I thought she was just being paranoid again. She's been treating everyone so awfully since Marcia—well, you know."

"It appears she wasn't imaging things this time," Luke said grimly.

"Maybe it was the stuffed pepper," Tess said hopefully. "You heard Cail say they'd never agreed with her."

"Why would she eat them if she knows that?" Luke asked.

"She might have done it to spite Cail," Lila said. "He told her not to order stuffed peppers, so that's what she ordered. He should stop saying anything to Heather. She puts the worst connotation on every word."

"Speaking of Cail," Tess said, "have you ever heard him mention a Chuck or Buck, Lida? I think it's somebody he plays pool with at the Red Dog."

Luke was staring at her. Oops, she probably

121

shouldn't have mentioned the Red Dog in his hearing. And she mustn't waste much more time in telling Chief Butts about what she learned there. From a drunk. She wouldn't mention that part to Butts.

"Cail never mentioned anybody like that to me," Lida said curtly. Then she jumped up as the doctor parted the curtains around Heather's cubicle and strode toward them.

"We've pumped her stomach," he said, "just in case she hadn't already gotten rid of everything."

"Was—was she poisoned?" Tess queried. Heather had told everybody within earshot that she'd been poisoned when they wheeled her into the emergency room.

"We won't know the results of the screen for a day or two. Even then, we can't be sure. The screen only detects a few of the more common poisons. It could take literally dozens of tests to pick up a poison not accounted for in the screen, if indeed she *was* poisoned. We will, however, know whether or not it was food contaminated by E. coli or salmonella."

"How is she?" Luke asked.

"She's going to be all right, I think. We'll keep her here a day or two to be sure." The doctor looked from Lida to Tess. "Which one of you is Tess?"

"I am."

"Miss Brackland wants a word with you before we take her up to her room."

All three of them started toward the cubicle. "You two will have to wait here," the doctor said. "She asked to speak to Tess alone."

Heather's face was almost as pale as the sheet that was pulled up to her chin. With her eyes closed, she could have been a corpse. Perhaps she almost had been.

"Heather?"

Her eyes flew open, panic registering in her expression. "Oh, it's you, Tess."

"The doctor said you wanted to talk to me."

She raked fingers through her tangled hair. Her hand was shaking. "I need you to do something for me."

"Sure, anything."

"Get my computer and camera out of my room and take them to your apartment."

"Your broken camera?"

Heather closed her eyes for a moment, her bottom lip trembling. "No, I bought a new one. It's in the bottom drawer of the dresser, under the T-shirts."

"Okay. I'll get them as soon as I get back to Iris House."

"Also, there's a folder containing some computer printouts and a computer disk in the linen closet, under the towels. Would you take those, too?"

"Yes."

Heather's hand shot out from under the sheet and she grasped Tess's hand. "Hide my things in a safe place, Tess." She was squeezing Tess's hand so hard, Tess winced. Heather didn't seem to notice. "No matter what they say, don't let anyone else get their hands on that material. Let nobody know you have my things. *Nobody*, Tess."

With difficulty, Tess extricated her hand from Heather's desperate grip. "Don't worry. I'll take care of it."

Heather raised up on one elbow. "This is important, Tess," she persisted. "You may not be safe if they find out you have my things."

"Nobody will know."

"I just thought of something else. If any mail comes for me, hide that, too."

"I will."

Heather studied her face intently for a long moment and finally lay back, satisfied. Tess could see her hands moving beneath the sheet, as though Heather were repeatedly clasping and unclasping them.

Tess hated to leave her in such an anxious state. "The doctor says you'll be fine."

"For now," Heather said, her voice barely above a whisper, "but they'll try again." She sounded almost resigned to the fate she was convinced was looming in her near future.

"Who will try again?"

"The killer, the one who murdered Marcia. He must have put something in my food when I left the table to go to the ladies' room."

"You still think it was Cail?" Tess wished she could reassure Heather of her safety, but if the food was poisoned, Tess's money was on Cail, even though she had been so sure the killer wouldn't risk trying again. He'd have to be incredibly desperate, she'd told Gertie. Well, if the poison test came back positive, it seemed he *was* desperate.

Heather didn't respond for a moment. Finally, she said, "I'm not sure any more who it is. I have information that could get Cail in big trouble. But the Hansels keep watching me like a couple of vultures; they're really worried I might print something else about them. And Pat Snell—" She sighed heavily. "I don't know what her problem is, but she can't stand the sight of me."

"Who were you sitting by at dinner tonight?"

Heather frowned. "Kent Hansel was on one side and Dorinda was on the other. It couldn't have been either of them, but any of the others could have done it, Tess. People kept getting up and going to the rest room. It would've been easy to drop something in my food as they passed my place."

Wanting to get her mind off who might be trying to kill her, Tess asked, "Is there anything else I can do for you?"

"Tell the police what happened. Maybe they'll post a guard on my hospital room."

"I'll call Chief Butts first thing in the morning," Tess assured her, though she doubted Butts could spare an officer to guard Heather's door when they weren't even sure she'd been poisoned. "And I'll come back to see you tomorrow. Maybe they'll release you and I can take you home with me."

The panic was back in her eyes. "No! I can't leave here till the police catch the murderer."

Tess patted her shoulder. "Try to get some rest, Heather. I'll see you tomorrow."

On the drive back to Iris House, Lida asked from the back seat, "Tess, what did Heather want to talk to you about?"

"Nothing important," Tess said casually. "She wanted to apologize for vomiting on the foyer floor."

Luke, who was driving, glanced over at Tess and started to say something. Tess gave a tiny shake of her head. But as soon as they were back in Tess's apartment, and Lida had gone upstairs, he asked, "What did Heather really want?"

Tess had promised not to tell—Heather felt she would be in jeopardy if anybody knew she had Heather's things. But that "anybody" didn't include Luke. So she told him what Heather had said, and he went with her to the Carnaby Room to help carry down the items Heather wanted Tess to take for safekeeping.

Tess pulled a suitcase from the back of her bedroom closet, packed Heather's things inside, then locked the case and dropped the key into the pocket of her navy blazer.

"I guess it's too late to talk to the Hansels tonight," Tess said.

"Yeah, everybody's asleep by now," Luke agreed. "It's one-fifteen. We can do it first thing tomorrow."

Chapter 19

Rudy was clearly glad for the interruption when, early the next morning, Tess asked him and Lillith if they could skip their walk and come into the apartment for a few minutes. Kent wanted to come, too, but Rudy told him to go with Lida and Cail.

Tess had placed a tray with a coffeepot and several mugs on the coffee table. She introduced the couple to Luke, who poured coffee for the Hansels, then sat down in a chair facing the sofa, where Rudy and Lillith sat.

Tess went to her office, returning with the film canister in a plastic bag. "My housekeeper found this in your wastebasket. I wanted you to be aware of it before I turn it over to the police."

Lillith turned pale. Characteristically, Rudy began to bluster. "Is your housekeeper in the habit of going through your guests' trash?"

"She just happened to see this when she emptied your basket."

"I could make a case that this is invasion of privacy."

Refusing to be put on the defensive, Tess merely waited. Finally, Rudy tried another tack. "Hell, Tess, what would the police want with an exposed roll of film? I've had that roll for a long time. I was afraid it wasn't any good, so I tossed it. I need to pick up another roll."

Tess turned the canister to see the date on the side. "The expiration date is July third," she said. "That's four months in the future, Rudy."

Luke inserted, "Besides, Tess was under the impression you didn't bring a camera with you."

Lillith reached out and took her husband's hand in both of hers—clutched it, actually.

"Well, she's wrong!" Rudy snapped.

"Am I, Rudy?" Tess asked. "When my guests bring a camera, they usually take it with them every time they go out. I've never seen you or Lillith with a camera."

Lillith looked at Rudy, who squeezed his wife's hand and said, "I suppose you're going to tell me your housekeeper searched our suite and didn't find a camera."

"No, she didn't search," Tess said quietly. "The only reason she brought this to me is that she heard Heather saying somebody had stolen the film from her camera before they destroyed it. She thought this might be that roll of film, and I think she's right. The police will dust it for fingerprints, and if they find Heather's . . ."

Rudy pulled his hand from Lillith's and set down his coffee, which he hadn't touched. He stood and rammed his hands into the pockets of his walking shorts, which Tess noticed peripherially were already a little looser at the waist.

Luke moved to the edge of his chair, evidently to be prepared in case Rudy decided to get physical. Rudy stepped a couple paces from the sofa, turned, and faced Tess. "All right. I took the film, and I smashed the camera."

"No, Rudy . . ." Lillith murmured.

He raised his voice, drowning her out. "That woman was snapping pictures of me and my family all over the place. Before and after shots, my ass! She was planning another story on us. I'm not sorry I destroyed her camera. I'd do it again! If that rag prints another word about me or my family, I'll sue their pants off. And I may charge your housekeeper with invasion of privacy while I'm at it!" He balled his hands into fists and positioned his feet some distance apart in an aggressive stance. His eyes were blazing.

Luke unfolded his six-feet-plus and went to stand beside Tess's chair. "Why don't you calm down, pal?"

Lillith rose, too, and moved to her husband's side. "Please don't upset yourself, honey." She turned to Tess and Luke, her face still pale but her chin lifted bravely. "He's protecting me. I'm the one who took the film, and I used one of Lida's dumbbells on the camera. Rudy was in such a stew about the pictures. I worry about his blood pressure. I wanted to remove the source of his distress."

Rudy put a protective arm around her. "We just want to be left alone, dammit. Do you really have to tell the police any of this?"

"I can't withhold evidence in a criminal investigation, Rudy."

"Look, I admit Lillith shouldn't have done it, but at worst she's guilty of poor judgment. It's just a camera, for God's sake. I'll replace it. Why can't we leave the police out of this?"

"Because," Tess told him, "Heather thinks whoever destroyed her camera killed Marcia, mistaking her for Heather. You heard her tell the police that."

"Oh, dear God . . ." The trace of color left in Lillith's face drained out of it, and she sagged against her husband.

Rudy's arm wrapped around her shoulders. "That's ridiculous! Lillith wouldn't hurt a fly. She didn't even mind the story Heather wrote about our wedding. I'm the one who raised a ruckus."

Lillith might not have cared about the wedding story, but Tess had seen her reaction when Heather threatened the Hansels—saying that she could get "all kinds of proof about many things."

Heather had sounded so vengeful, that Tess could remember her exact words. *You should know about being ruined, right, Rudy?* And when Lillith had called her an evil person, Heather had lashed out: *You're no angel yourself, Barbie!* Tess didn't know what Heather had meant by the seeming threats, but she was beginning to think she should find out. If Heather was threatening to write something else about the Hansels, it had to be much worse than the wedding story, for Heather's words had clearly terrified Lillith. Would Lillith resort to murder to shut Heather up?

"I'm sorry," Tess said finally, "but I must turn the film over to the police. I'm sure they'll be contacting you."

Rudy glared at her, then at Luke. "Come on, Lillith," he said finally. "There's nothing more to be said here." As they walked past Tess and Luke, he added a parting shot. "Don't expect us to recommend Iris House to our friends."

He led his wife out of the apartment and slammed the door.

Tess released a held breath. "That man can fly off the handle in an instant. I'm glad you were here, Luke."

"Yeah, me too," Luke mused.

"Do you think Lillith could have killed Marcia?"

Luke shrugged. "Rudy's a much more likely candidate, but—" He paused for an instant, then added, "she *did* use a dumbbell on Heather's camera."

"I wonder if it was the same one that killed Marcia," Tess pondered.

"Maybe when you talk to Butts, he'll at least tell you if they found any prints on the dumbbell."

"Maybe," Tess said doubtfully. "But most of the guests have used the dumbbells. Prints wouldn't be much help."

"I have to get to the office, love."

Tess kissed him goodbye and went to phone Chief Butts. Then she sat down to wait.

The guests would be back for breakfast very soon. Lida would have already told them Heather would be all right, but Tess thought about going out to add her reassurances. Then she dismissed the thought. Clearly she was no longer the proprietor of a bed and breakfast full of guests. She was the proprietor of a bed and breakfast full of murder suspects.

Tess thought about them in turn.

Rudy and Lillith were hiding something, something they didn't want Heather to plaster all over *The National Scoop*. Lillith was terrified and Rudy was furious. Either emotion could be an impetus for murder.

Pat Snell was intent on making sure Heather had no photographs of her. What her motivation was, Tess couldn't fathom. *The Scoop* didn't carry articles about ordinary citizens unless their story was really bizarre—like a claim that they'd been abducted by aliens or talked to the dead. And what had Pat ever done that was worthy of tabloid coverage? Which left Tess with a big question mark. *Why* had Pat been so disturbed about Heather's picture-taking?

Lida Darnell was having an affair with Cail and seemed to feel threatened by any other woman who showed an interest in him. Cail may have told her about Heather's attempt at blackmail. Would she commit murder to protect him? Tess didn't want to think so, but Lida wouldn't be the first woman to murder for love.

Cail Marrs was apparently wanted for questioning by the Los Angeles police. And, according to Heather, he owed her money, which she had been trying to collect by threatening to notify the California authorities where they could find Cail. He certainly had a strong motive to want Heather silenced. Though he wasn't staying at Iris House, he hadn't been at home at the time Marcia was killed. He would remain at the top of Tess's list of suspects. Dorinda Fenster and Kent Hansel seemed to be the only occupants of Iris House who had *no* motive to want Heather out of the way. Of the two, only Kent had been outside the night Marcia was killed. But so had all the others.

As had Donnie Armory. Tess made a mental note to talk to Donnie again. Perhaps he'd remembered something else about the night he found Marcia's body.

Chapter 20

Desmond Butts sat at Tess's kitchen table, taking notes as Tess told him about Lillith's admission that she'd destroyed Heather's camera. She had already turned over the film Lillith had removed from the camera. She went on to tell him of Heather's claim that somebody had tried to poison her, adding that the doctor had not been willing to venture a guess as to why Heather had become ill after eating stuffed peppers for dinner. He was waiting for the results of a poison screen, which might or might not solve the dilemma.

"Nutty woman," Butts muttered in disgust.

Tess poured him a cup of coffee, then sat down across the table from him. "Heather does seem to be overreacting to a lot of things, Chief Butts, but she's terrified. She wants you to put a guard on her door at the hospital."

Butts ignored the suggestion. "I'll have a talk with the doctor. Could be just a nervous stomach or something."

Tess did not know what a nervous stomach was, and she didn't care to ask. "I assume you'll be talking to the Hansels, too."

"Soon as I leave here." He picked up his coffee cup, took a swallow, made a face, and studied Tess. Butts was dour, set in his ways, a lifelong resident of Victoria Springs who liked the town much better before it had become a tourist destination. All those outsiders pouring in made his job a lot harder. He especially disliked situations that required him to deal with the rich ones who looked upon the local police as part of the servant class, like their housekeepers back home. Tess was sure Butts had already placed the Hansels in that category. Those who opened bed and breakfast inns to accommodate the hordes of outsiders weren't among his favorite people, either.

So it surprised Tess when he volunteered, "That dumbbell had been wiped clean of prints, but we found a trace of the victim's blood. According to the M.E., she died of blunt trauma to the head. The dumbbell's the murder weapon, all right. Not that there was ever much doubt."

"Have you released the body yet?"

He shook his head. "I'm gonna have the morgue hold on to it a couple more days before I tell the sister she can have it. If she leaves, it might make the others think they can go, too."

Poor Dorinda. Butts had no qualms at all about forcing her to delay the funeral, which Tess felt Dorinda would have to get through before she could begin to put her sister's death behind her.

"Have you talked to Donnie Armory?"

Butts pursed his mouth into a miserly line. "The kid was useless. He was too scared to notice anything but the fact that there was a woman laying out in the rain who wouldn't get up."

Tess suspected Butts had intimidated the boy. "Maybe I can find out if he's remembered anything else since you talked to him."

He studied her again. "Yeah, maybe you can. If you learn anything else, bring it straight to me. Don't give the information to Struthers like you did the tip about Heather Brackland blackmailing Cail Hurst."

"So his name *is* Hurst?"

"We ran Marrs and Hurst through the computer. There's an outstanding warrant in California for Cail Hurst. Drug dealing."

"So you'll be notifying the California authorities."

"Not yet," Butts said. "I don't want him to leave town till this case is wrapped up. If I find enough evidence to arrest him, California will probably waive extradition. And don't you be warning him we know about the California warrant."

"I would never do that, Chief. You should know me better than that by now."

He snorted. "Guess I should, Tess, the way you keep popping up at murder scenes."

Tess sighed. "I'd prefer not to, believe me."

He made a noncommital sound. "I like Cail Hurst— or Marrs—whatever—for this murder, Tess. I figure if I give him enough rope, he'll hang himself. Which is why I don't want him to know we're on to him." His bushy brows rose and he waited, as if he expected a response.

"My lips are sealed," Tess assured him.

He fixed her with the intimidating look he must use when questioning suspected criminals. "Anything else you want to tell me, Tess?"

"There is one thing," she admitted. "The night Marcia was killed, Lida tried to call Cail in his apartment until well after midnight. He wasn't there."

He nodded. "We're already trying to trace his movements that night."

"I know he was at the Red Dog saloon until about eleven-thirty. He paid a man named Chuck or Buck to make a phone call for him. I couldn't learn anything else about that phone call, but it was made about the time Heather received the threatening call."

Butts grunted. "How did you come by this information?"

"I—I'd rather not say, but this Chuck—or Buck—is a regular at the Red Dog. I'm sure you can track him down."

"I will, and you keep your nose out of it. This Cail is a nasty character, Tess, so be real careful you don't tip him off."

Tess couldn't suppress a shudder. "I said I wouldn't."

She wondered if she dared press her luck any further
and decided she had nothing to lose. "You said you were
going to check into Marcia Yoder's background."

"Nothing there, Tess," he said impatiently. "She lived
in Seattle till her divorce, when she moved to Denver.
Her sister gave me her address and I contacted the Denver police. They sent a man out to talk to Yoder's neigh-
bors. A couple of 'em said she'd gotten kind of strange
lately, had some weird-looking friends, but as far as they
knew she had no enemies. Her sister said the same. No,
the killer was after Heather Brackland."

What Butts had learned seemed to remove any doubt
about that. When the killer saw a woman wearing
Heather's raincoat in the dim light from the yard lamps,
he thought he'd found his target.

Tess remembered the crime scene tape and said, "By
the way, can I remove that yellow tape from the backyard now?"

"Yeah, we're through out there." Butts closed his tablet and stuck it in his shirt pocket. "Where can I find the
Hansels?"

"In the dining room. They'll still be at breakfast."

"Good. I don't like that Rudy." No surprise to Tess.
"So I'm gonna throw a real good scare into him." He
stood and clomped out of the kitchen.

"Remember, Tess," he said at the door, "No talking
about police business to anybody."

How many times did he think he had to tell her?
Hadn't she already proved she could keep her own counsel? After all, it was only a month ago that she'd helped
him solve a murder at the senior citizens center. How
soon Butts had forgotten.

"Got it, Chief," she said dryly.

Tess went immediately to the backyard and took down
the yellow tape, rolling it up and tossing it into the trash
barrel in the alley behind the back fence. Though the
alley was graveled, there were big patches of bare dirt,
one of them next to the back gate.

Remembering that Marcia's killer could have escaped
the backyard by way of the alley, it should have oc-

curred to her before now to look around there.

It had been raining the night of the murder. The spots in the alley where the gravel had been worn away would have been wet and soft. If the killer left this way, he would surely have left footprints. There were plenty of tire tracks from the trash hauler's truck, which came down the alley twice a week. There were even a few discernible footprints near the tire tracks, probably left by the men who jumped off the truck to empty the trash barrels. But the dirt patch on the alley side of the back gate was smooth—no tracks.

If the murderer had left by the alley, he'd have had to walk across that patch of dirt, which would have been mud that night. Since there were no footprints, the murderer couldn't have made his escape this way. He'd gone around the side of the house to the front. If it was Cail, as Butts suspected, he'd have parked his car nearby, and had managed to get to it and drive away without being seen.

Tess went back through the gate and entered the house through the back door. Gertie was clearing the breakfast table, and the guests, all except Lillith and Rudy, were moving the furniture into place for the morning support session.

Tess made her breakfast, toast and a glass of orange juice, which she ate at the kitchen table.

"What's Chief Butts talking to the Hansels about?" Gertie asked in a low voice, as she arranged dirty dishes in the dishwasher.

"I've been ordered not to discuss police business with anyone," Tess told her.

Gertie shook her head. "Well, if you ask me, it'll be a good day when this bunch leaves. At breakfast they were talking about Heather Brackland being in the hospital, said she claimed she was poisoned." She looked questioningly at Tess.

"The doctor isn't sure. He's waiting for test results."

Butts was closeted with the Hansels in the suite for twenty minutes. When Tess heard him stomping down the stairs, she went to the foyer, hoping he'd tell her about his talk with the couple. But he merely stalked past her and left the house, a thunderous expression on his broad face. Tess thought Rudy had probably threatened him with a lawsuit, as he'd already threatened Heather and Tess.

The Hansels didn't join the group until lunchtime. Rudy looked gray and exhausted, and it was obvious that Lillith had been crying. The other guests watched the couple covertly, and most of the meal passed in silence.

Tess waited until the group had finished their lunch to have her own. In her apartment, she set a bowl of vegetable soup and a large glass of milk on a tray and carried it to the sitting room. Settling on the sofa beside Primrose, she clicked on the television set to watch part of a talk show while she ate.

As she reached for the glass, she caught a glimpse of something shiny in her peripheral vision. Looking closer, she saw the spine of a book, which had slipped down between the arm of the sofa and the cushion. She pulled it out.

It was Dr. Patrice Singleton's book, the one her guests were reading and discussing. How had this copy landed there? It was a moment before she remembered. Heather had been carrying the book the day after the murder when she'd come to Tess's apartment. This had to be the same book because Tess didn't have a copy and nobody else had brought one to the apartment.

She laid the book on the coffee table. Heather certainly had no need for the book now. Tess would return it to Lida later.

After lunch, she went out to check on the construction project. Donnie was sitting on the grass, near where his father and the other men were building the framework for the walls. The boy seemed absorbed in whatever he held in his hand. As Tess drew closer, she saw that it was a small electronic game.

"Hi, Donnie," Tess greeted him.

He looked up. "Oh, hi, Miss Darcy."

Heedless of staining the seat of her jeans, she sat

down beside him. The small screen in Donnie's hand displayed a ball player holding a baseball bat. Balls shot up from the bottom of the screen at intervals.

"Are you winning?" Tess asked.

"I'm not doing real good today. My batting average is just 300."

Not being a baseball fan, Tess wasn't sure exactly what that meant. "You feeling OK?"

He turned off the game and the screen went blank. "Yeah, I guess. Dad told me that lady I found in your backyard was dead."

"Yes," Tess admitted.

"The police chief asked me a lot of questions. He acted like it made him mad 'cause I couldn't answer them. He kept saying I must have seen somebody else in the backyard, but I didn't, Tess. Honest. I told my Dad the same thing when he asked me later."

"Sometimes," Tess said, "Chief Butts pushes a little too hard."

"My Dad finally told him to leave me alone."

"I'm sorry to keep talking about this, Donnie, but I thought you might have remembered something else about that night after you talked to Chief Butts and your dad. Did you hear a car or anything like that?"

He thought about it. "No, I didn't hear anything."

Which could mean he was so frightened he didn't hear the car. Or there was nothing to hear—Cail might have parked several blocks away and walked to Iris House. Or it wasn't Cail, after all, and the killer had simply returned to Iris House.

Donnie watched her for a moment. "I didn't hear anything, and I didn't see anybody."

"All right, Donnie."

"But I was thinking about it again last night, and I remembered seeing something sparkling."

"Sparkling? What do you mean?"

"It was like a flash, but when I looked closer it was gone."

"A flash? Like a flashlight or a flashbulb on a camera?"

"No, it wasn't that big. Just a little flash." He shrugged, unable to give a more specific description.

"Could it have been light from one of the yard lamps reflecting off metal or glass?"

He frowned. "I don't know, I guess so. It was so dark, I can't say for sure."

"Do you think you could show me where you saw the flash?"

"Maybe."

Wayne Armory had sent several glances their way, and now he walked over to them. "What are you two talking about?"

"Donnie says he saw a flash the night he found Marcia Yoder. Is it all right if he shows me where he saw it?"

Wayne looked closely at his son's face. "You never mentioned that to the police."

"I didn't remember it till later, Dad."

"It's probably nothing, Wayne," Tess added.

"Well, go ahead and show Tess, if you want to," Wayne said.

Although the crime scene tape had been removed and there was nothing left to indicate where the body had been, Donnie went straight to the spot and faced north. "I found the lady about here, and the flash was over there." He pointed toward the wrought-iron fence where shrubs ran along the north fence line. "It was too dark over there to see the fence or the bushes." He looked at Tess. "I'm pretty sure I didn't imagine it, Miss Darcy."

"Was the flash near the ground, or higher up?"

He walked nearer the fence. "It was right about there." He lifted his arm, indicating a spot slightly above his head.

"Thank you, Donnie. Now, how would you like one of Gertie's brownies?"

"That'd be great!"

Tess took him into the house. Gertie had put the iced, nut-filled brownies in a bread box in the pantry, to keep them from tempting the guests.

Tess gave Donnie one. He grinned and licked a bit of icing off his fingers. "My mom usually packs me a snack, but Kent's been talking me out of 'em. He says he'll starve to death if I don't give him something."

"Since you're giving away the snacks, maybe you should tell your mother not to send them. Kent is on a restricted diet, but I can guarantee he's not going to die of starvation."

"Good idea," Donnie agreed.

WITCH DEAD

Chapter 21

After Donnie went back outside with his brownie, Tess stood at the window over the kitchen sink, looking out at the backyard. Had Donnie seen a flash, or was it just a figment of a frightened boy's fertile imagination?

Not a flashlight or a flashbulb, Donnie had seemed pretty sure about that. Something not as big, he'd said. Tess scanned the shrubs where Donnie had seen the flash. There was nothing in the area that light could have reflected off of, producing the "flash" Donnie described. But what if somebody had been standing there, wearing something that might have reflected the light. Jewelry? It didn't seem likely it was jewelry, unless it contained a very large stone. A diamond could have produced such a flash. Tess had never seen Cail wear any jewelry. In fact, the only jewelry she'd noticed on any of the guests was Lillith's wedding band. Tess discarded the jewelry idea for the moment.

What else might reflect light? A gun came to mind, but the killer probably hadn't had a gun. The noise of a gunshot would have roused this quiet neighborhood and, besides, the murderer had brought a dumbbell to use as a weapon.

"Tess?"

Tess jumped a foot off the floor at the voice

close behind her. She steadied herself by grabbing the
edge of the counter, took a deep breath and turned
around.

"Sorry," Pat Snell said. "I didn't mean to scare you."

"I guess I'm a little jumpy today."

"Aren't we all!" Pat ran a finger under the nose piece
of her eyeglasses and massaged gently. "These new
frames are driving me crazy. They're rubbing a sore spot
on the side of my nose."

Tess stared at her. It was a moment before she realized
Pat was still talking.

"—er . . . what did you say?" Tess asked.

"I came down to get some tomato juice."

"It's in the refrigerator," Tess told her. "Help yourself."

Pat took out a can of juice and left the kitchen with
it. Tess watched her go as she absorbed the thought that
had struck her when Pat began rubbing the sore spot on
her nose. Eyeglass lenses could easily reflect light at
night, and Pat Snell was the only one of the guests who
wore glasses.

Tess had never thought very seriously of Pat Snell as
a potential murderer. Yet Pat had vehemently protested
Heather's picture-taking, more than once. And Heather
said Pat couldn't stand the sight of her, but why, other
than the fact that Heather worked for an unsavory tabloid? Would Pat actually try to kill Heather over a snapshot?

Maybe Heather knew something incriminating about
Pat, something bad enough to warrant an article in a
tabloid. Trying to conjure up something about Pat Snell
was difficult. She appeared to be quite an ordinary
woman.

Still, it was worth pursuing. What could be so terrible
that Pat didn't want Heather repeating it? Tess had no
idea what that might be. But if Heather did possess such
knowledge, she could have made a note of it on her
computer and it might be among the printouts in the
folder Tess had hidden along with Heather's computer
and camera.

She really had no right to look at Heather's private notes. It was a pure invasion of privacy. She always made a point to give her guests as much privacy as possible. But sometimes there was a higher priority than privacy—catching a murderer, for example.

Tess struggled with her conscience, but only briefly.

Heather's folder contained several pages of computer printouts. Tess took the folder to the kitchen table to read them.

On top was a page containing a summary of Rudy Hansel's background and career. The second page contained a similar summary on Lillith.

On the third page was what appeared to be the body of an article.

Real estate tycoon, Rudy Hansel, recently married for the second time to supermodel Lillith, is reportedly having serious financial problems. In fact, his real estate holdings, much of them in California, are mortgaged to the hilt. California real estate values have plummeted in the last year, and, according to a reliable source, several banks have called for repayment of Hansel's loans.

Rumor has it that Hansel has contacted his attorney about starting bankruptcy proceedings.

Looks like Hansel may even have to sell off some or all of his residences. And Lillith may have to come out of retirement to help pay the bills.

The article ended there. It certainly explained Heather's angry remark to Rudy, when he threatened to ruin her. *You know all about being ruined, don't you, Rudy?* she'd retorted.

No wonder Rudy was so irate over Heather's picture-taking. Tess could easily imagine a snapshot of Rudy at the weight-loss retreat. The caption might read: REAL ESTATE TYCOON RUDY HANSEL SHAPES UP AT EXPENSIVE RETREAT WHILE HIS TEETERING EMPIRE CRUMBLES. Heather could cause Rudy's financial woes to be mul-

tiplied. Banks that hadn't already demanded payment
might do so if *The National Scoop* ran this.

Tess put the article aside and picked up the next prin-
tout. The brief note read:

No Pat Snell or Patricia Snell in Topeka phone directory and
information doesn't have an unlisted number. Check of Kansas drivers' licenses turned up no Pat or Patricia Snell.

Deon@nationalscoop.com

Apparently Heather had had him check Pat's background. How intriguing. For some reason, Heather had
become suspicious of Pat's story that she ran a craft mall
in Topeka.

Tess stared out the kitchen window, only vaguely
aware of the men working on the new addition. Why
was Heather suspicious of Pat? In fact, why had she
cared enough to have somebody at the tabloid check Pat
out? Pat wasn't a well-known personality—there seemed
little likelihood that she would warrant a story in *The
National Scoop*.

Even more curious was the fact that Pat seemed to
have lied about where she lived. Tess could think of no
reason for her to do that. Maybe this Deon had somehow
received misinformation. There ought to be another way
to find out if Pat had lied besides checking the official
records.

Tess thought a more direct approach might work. She
went to her office telephone, asked the operator for the
Topeka, Kansas area code, then dialed information and
requested the number of the Topeka Chamber of Commerce.

By the time somebody answered, she'd come up with
a story. "Hi. This is Sally Burns. I'm a freelance writer,
and I'm doing a story on craft malls in Kansas."

"Oh, yes, we have several here," the woman replied.
"They seem to be springing up all over the country. In
fact, my sister rents a booth. She makes doll clothes and
sells them at one of our malls."

"It certainly gives crafters another outlet for their handiwork, besides craft fairs which usually last only two or three days," Tess said smoothly. "I'm hoping you can give me the addresses and phone numbers of the craft malls in Topeka. I'd like to interview the managers for my article."

"Oh, sure," the woman said helpfully. "Let me get my file." She came back shortly and read off names, addresses, and phone numbers of four craft malls. "If you want to interview any crafters," she added, "I'm sure my sister would be happy to talk to you."

"Okay, give me your sister's name and phone number," Tess said. She even wrote down the information, knowing that she would not use it. "Thanks so much for your help."

Tess called all four craft malls, said that she was writing an article, and asked for the manager's name. None of them was Pat Snell. Two of the managers weren't available at the moment, but she talked to the other two, asked how many craft booths they had and which crafts seemed to sell the best, enough to satisfy them that her queries were legitimate. It turned out doll clothes were a hot item. If Tess had really been writing an article, she would definitely have contacted the sister of the woman who'd answered at the Chamber of Commerce.

Before ending the conversations, she asked both the managers she talked to if they knew a Pat Snell, whom she understood managed a craft mall in Topeka. Neither of the women had ever heard of Pat, and one said, "I know all the mall managers here, and she's not one of them. Maybe she's in Wichita."

"Perhaps I misunderstood," Tess said offhandedly and rang off.

She sat at her desk for several moments, pondering. Indeed, it did seem that Pat had lied, at least about what she did for a living, and from the e-mail in Heather's folder, it appeared Pat didn't even live in Topeka.

Now, why would anybody lie about that?

Actually, Tess could think of several potential reasons, all a bit outlandish, to be sure. Recently, she'd seen a television program on people who had managed to lose themselves somewhere in the country, far away from where they were known. One had been a divorced father, who was wanted by the authorities for failure to pay legally mandated child support. Another had been a woman who'd been part of a group who, years ago, had protested government intervention in the lives of individuals by bombing government buildings at night. A janitor had been killed in their last bombing, and all the group members, except the woman profiled on television, had been tried and convicted of murder more than twenty years ago. Some of them were still serving time in prison.

The subject of the profile had chosen to run away instead—had changed her name, moved to a remote village in Maine, married, and had two children. Then one day, somebody from her past had been passing through town, had caught sight of her at the post office, and notified the authorities. She'd been arrested, tried, and given a two-year jail sentence, which she was allowed to serve close to her home. The judge had shown leniency because of the exemplary life she'd led since her protest days.

Was Pat Snell a criminal in hiding?

Interesting thought, but Tess found it hard to credit. Still, Pat definitely had dyed hair, as Marcia had so bluntly pointed out during the group's attempt to play the "honesty game." Clearly Pat had wanted to change her looks. But it *was* a bit obvious. It didn't look like a professional coloring; perhaps Pat had done it herself.

But the person who'd made the comment was Marcia Yoder, not Heather. Still, Tess *had* heard Heather say more than once that Pat looked familiar to her. If Pat was in hiding, anything that called attention to her must make her very nervous. Heather's repeatedly trying to place where she'd seen Pat before might drive her to desperation.

Tess found this line of thought intriguing, but it was pure speculation. She decided it was time to visit Heather in the hospital again. Perhaps she had remembered where she'd seen Pat before.

Chapter 22

Heather was sitting up in her hospital bed, leafing through a magazine, which she tossed aside when she saw Tess.

"Come in and close the door," Heather said urgently.

Tess did as she asked, then pulled a chair up beside the bed. "How are you feeling?"

Heather darted a worried glance toward the door as muffled footsteps passed in the hallway. "I'm a nervous wreck, Tess. The doctor was just here and they found arsenic in the poison test." She clutched Tess's hand. "*Arsenic*, Tess!"

For a moment, Tess was too stunned for words. She had almost convinced herself that the killer wouldn't dare try again, that it was the green pepper that had made Heather ill. She tried to hide her dismay. Heather was already agitated enough.

"But you seem all right now, and I'm sure the hospital will report the findings to the police."

"Yes, the doctor said they were required by law to do so." Heather continued to hold Tess's hand in a death grip.

"I'm sure Chief Butts will be by to see you today. Just let the police handle it, Heather."

"At least *now* Butts might put a guard on my door. I'm absolutely terrified that the murderer will try again."

146

Tess extracted her hand, noticing that Heather had placed the control box for signaling the nurse on the bed within easy reach. "You'll be safe here," she said reassuringly.

Heather closed her eyes. "The doctor said I wasn't sick enough to have received a lethal dose of the poison. Whoever gave it to me evidently didn't know how much to use. He won't make the same mistake a second time."

"Maybe he just wanted to scare you, not kill you," Tess said, trying to put the best spin on a horrifying situation.

Heather opened her eyes, which were dull and red-rimmed. She probably hadn't slept much last night. "He murdered Marcia, thinking it was me, Tess. He wants to kill me all right."

"Where do you suppose he got arsenic?" Tess pondered.

"According to the doctor, it's in rat poison and pesticides. Anybody can buy that stuff over the counter. Half the houses in town could have something containing arsenic. Do you have anything like that at Iris House?"

Tess shook her head. "We use a lawn service. They bring their own equipment and sprays."

"You know what I've been thinking, ever since the doctor was here?"

"What?"

"Lida could have something containing arsenic at the fitness center."

The same thought had occurred to Tess. It was possible, she supposed, for any one of her guests to have gotten to town, bought the poison, and returned during one of the two daily breaks in the retreat schedule. But surely they'd realize the police might check with stores that sold rodent poison and pesticides and get a description of the buyer. However, if they had arsenic at the center, both Lida and Cail already had access.

"I convinced the doctor to let me stay here another night or two," Heather said, "but after that they'll kick me out. My insurance won't pay for an extended stay.

I'll go back to Iris House long enough to pack my things, and then I'm going home."

Tess didn't blame her. In Heather's place, she'd want to leave Victoria Springs as soon as possible. But how safe would she be back in L.A.? If the killer was determined . . .

Heather wouldn't really be safe until the murderer was caught. "Would you like me to pack for you? I could keep your things in my apartment until you're ready to leave."

"Oh, would you, Tess? I was really dreading having to go back there. I don't want to see any of those people ever again."

"I have an idea," Tess told her. "I'll tell everybody that you've left the hospital and gone to stay with a relative for a few days. That way, nobody will try to visit you."

Heather nodded. "Yes, and I can tell the nurse to put a "No Visitors" sign on my door."

Tess said hesitantly, "Heather, I've heard talk that Cail owes you money."

She made a face. "Pat blabbed, huh? She eavesdropped on a conversation I had with Cail. Well, it's no big secret. Cail and I bought a condo together in L.A. and he skipped out, leaving me to make the full payment."

"I was just thinking—it might be a good idea to call Cail, tell him you're going to stay with an aunt or something, and say you've decided not to try to collect the money he owes you."

She was silent for a long moment before she sighed and said, "I can't let him get away with this, Tess. It's not right. But I'll let up on it for a while. I feel too weak right now to fight Cail over the money." She closed her eyes for a moment, then opened them and said wearily, "If he won't pay me what he owes, I'll probably have to let the condo go back to the mortgage company. My credit will be ruined."

Better to lose the condo than to be dead, Tess thought. Heather watched her, as though trying to read her thoughts. "It's Cail who's trying to kill me, isn't it, Tess?"

Tess was tempted to tell her that she should be more careful who she tried to blackmail, but Heather was in no shape to handle criticism at the moment. "I honestly don't know, but the police are working on tracking down his whereabouts the night Marcia was killed. Also, Lillith has confessed to stealing your film and ruining your camera. She swears that's all she did, though. She was worried about Rudy because he was so upset by your picture-taking."

Heather's red-rimmed eyes widened. "Lillith!"

"Rudy said he'd pay for your camera, so you should send him a bill."

"I will, believe me!" For an instant, her fighting spirit returned, but it quickly drained out of her. "Right now, though, I have worse things to worry about."

"Perhaps you shouldn't write anything else about the Hansels, Heather."

She frowned. "I'll wait until after they arrest somebody for Marcia's murder before I decide that. I have to make a living, Tess."

Tess feared if she said any more about the Hansels, Heather would realize Tess had read her notes. "I don't want Chief Butts to know this, but I decided to do a little checking up on the guests myself. I started with Pat Snell. I even called all the craft malls in Topeka. Nobody's ever heard of her."

Briefly, interest flashed in Heather's eyes, but when she spoke, her tone was bleak. "She's hiding something, but I don't know what. Right now I couldn't care less. I'm not even sure it's worth pursuing."

Tess had only just convinced herself it *was* worth pursuing. "Pat dyed her hair," she prompted.

"Right, but what does that mean? Maybe she just got tired of the natural color. Women dye their hair all the time."

"The color isn't very flattering," Tess ventured. "I've been wondering if it's to disguise her appearance."

Heather frowned. "Like she doesn't want to be recognized, you mean?" The reporter's curiosity returned for a moment. "That could be. I know she doesn't need those glasses. I saw them lying on a table in the guest parlor and put them on. The lenses are plain glass."

"That's odd," Tess mused. Pat didn't need the glasses, yet she continued to wear them, even though they were rubbing a sore spot on her nose. "I heard you say she looked familiar to you. Have you remembered where you might have seen her before?"

Heather shook her head. "I've racked my brain and I can't place her. What are you thinking, Tess?"

"I have no idea why Pat has changed her appearance," Tess admitted.

"Maybe she's in hiding from an abusive husband or lover."

"Coming to a weight-loss retreat in a tourist town seems like a strange place to hide," Heather said.

"Losing weight could be part of her disguise."

"Yeah, I guess so." Heather seemed to have lost interest in Pat and her reason for disguising her appearance.

"You need to get some rest," Tess said. "Why don't you ask the nurse to give you a sleeping pill?"

Heather's expression was one of disbelief. "You can't be serious. I'm afraid to go to sleep, Tess."

"You have to sleep," Tess said gently. "I'm going back home to spread the word that you're leaving town. Call me at Iris House if you need anything."

"OK. When you go by the nurses' station, please tell somebody I want a 'No Visitors' sign on my door."

As Tess was leaving the nurses' station, after delivering Heather's message, Chief Butts got off the elevator at the end of the hall. He wore a fierce frown and stared at the tile floor in front of him. He didn't see Tess until he was upon her.

"Hello, Chief."

He halted. "Tess. You here visiting the Brackland woman?"

Tess nodded. "She's beside herself with fear, Chief.

Her doctor told her the poison screen picked up traces of arsenic."

"Yeah, I just heard from the doc." Frown lines creased his wide brow. "I gotta get this guy before he tries again."

"Heather and I decided I should tell everybody at Iris House that she's leaving town to stay with a relative. That should keep the killer from trying anything while she's in the hospital. I'll pack her things and keep them in my apartment until the doctor discharges her."

"Keep it under your hat that they found arsenic till I can get some search warrants."

"You're going to search Iris House?"

"If I can get the warrant—also, the fitness center and Cail Hurst's apartment. I'm going to the judge as soon as I leave here."

The idea of the police rummaging through Iris House set Tess's teeth on edge, even though she understood why Butts felt it should be done. It could tarnish her bed and breakfast's reputation as an elegant and private retreat. "If you get a warrant for Iris House, I'd appreciate it if you wouldn't broadcast it to the whole town."

He grunted a bit contemptuously. "I can't worry about your business, Tess. I've got a murder and an attempted murder on my hands here."

"I understand that. I'm just asking you to be discreet." Of course, asking Butts to be discreet was like asking a hard rock band to perform quietly.

His response was a snort of impatience. "Just don't let it slip about the warrants," he muttered and started past her.

"One other thing, Chief."

He turned back. "Huh?"

"I talked to Donnie Armory again. He remembers seeing a flash at the north side of the backyard when he found Marcia Yoder's body."

Butts looked skeptical. "What kind of flash?"

"He couldn't be very specific, except to say that it wasn't big enough to be a flashlight or a camera flashbulb. He just saw it for a second, from the corner of his eye, and then it was gone."

Butts waved a dismissive hand. "A flash, right." Shaking his head, he proceeded down the hall toward Heather's room.

Chapter 23

As Tess drove down her street, she saw that the mail had been delivered. In this part of town, postal boxes were required to be at the curb. The door to the Iris House box was open and a package protruded from the box.

She rolled down her car window and extracted the mail before driving around to her parking space. The envelopes were addressed to Tess and contained monthly utility bills; the package was addressed to Heather Brackland. The padded mailer was torn along one side as though it had been caught in a postal machine, and some of the padding was showing.

Entering Iris House, Tess ran into Lida in the foyer, which provided her with the opportunity to drop a word about Heather. "I've just come from the hospital," Tess said.

"Oh, how is Heather?" Lida asked.

"Better. In fact, if I'd been much later, I'd have missed her. She's leaving town and will be staying with a relative for a while."

"A relative? Where?"

Tess studied Lida's expression of concern, wondering if it was genuine and why Lida wanted to know where Heather was going. Tess caught herself starting to read sinister meanings into the most casual remarks. "Heather didn't say," she said.

"She just asked me to pack her things. She'll send for them later."

"Well," Lida mused, "if she's leaving the hospital, they must not have found any poison."

Tess made a noncommital reply and, excusing herself, went to her apartment. She tossed the package on the kitchen table and laid the rest of the mail on her desk. Then she poured a glass of lemonade and took it to her office.

She got out her checkbook and had started to write a check for the water bill when the phone rang.

"Hi, cuz."

"Hello, Cinny."

"If you're going to be home for a while, I thought I'd drop by. Marge can handle the shop on her own for an hour or two. We need to talk."

"I'll be here, but what do we need to talk about?"

"Tell you when I see you," Cinny said lightly and hung up.

By the time Cinny arrived, Tess had the utility checks ready to mail, had brewed a pot of herbal tea, and arranged a plate of butter cookies and two teacups on the kitchen table.

Cinny breezed in, wearing an electric pink dress that managed to look sexy and businesslike at the same time. Her cheeks were flushed. Either she'd been running or she was excited about something.

Tess led the way to the kitchen. "Sit down and I'll pour our tea." Cinny nibbled on a cookie while Tess poured.

"Now," said Tess, "what's this all about?"

Cinny threw out her hands and caroled, "Ta da! I'm going to marry Cody."

"Oh, Cinny! I'm so happy for you." Tess jumped up to hug her cousin. She was sure Cinny didn't guess she already knew of Cody's proposal.

Cinny smiled contentedly. "Of course, we can't tell anybody but you and Luke yet. It's a secret for now. We'll make an official announcement in June—after your wedding. Mother's totally involved in that, and I don't want to distract her."

"How thoughtful of you," Tess said, laughing. "You wouldn't be thinking of eloping, would you?"

Cinny wrinkled her nose. "Cody suggested it, and I was tempted. But I just can't do it. Mother would never forgive me."

"That's true."

Cinny spooned sugar into her tea and stirred. "Now, let's talk about the shower Mother and I are going to throw you. Mother thinks we should have it at the country club. What do you think?"

"Any place is fine with me. By the way, Gertie wants to provide the refreshments."

"Wonderful. That's one worry off my mind. I'll have Mother clear it with the club manager. The chef is a bit touchy about loaning out his kitchen."

For the next fifteen minutes, they talked about Tess's bridal shower and Cinny took notes. Finally, Cinny tucked her notepad and pen into her purse and dropped it on the table. As she did so, her eye fell on the torn package Tess had brought in with the mail. "What's this?"

"Something for Heather Brackland. She asked me to keep her mail here until she can take it."

Cinny picked up the package and thrust her index finger through the tear on the side. "Feels like a videotape." Spreading the torn opening wider with two fingers, she read *Barbie's Playhouse*. What in the world —?"

"Oh, my Lord!" Tess snatched the package from Cinny's hands.

Cinny regarded her curiously. "What is it, Tess?"

Tess spread the opening and read the spine of the videotape for herself. *Barbie's Playhouse*. Barbie was the name Heather had called Lillith. "Sounds like an x-rated video."

"Porn?" Cinny giggled. "I guess we shouldn't be surprised. Heather couldn't have very good taste and work for that tabloid, could she? But I thought it was mostly men who watched these things."

Heather's threatening remark to Lillith was beginning to make sense to Tess. "I think," Tess mused, "this may be research for an article Heather is working on."

Tess went on to tell Cinny about the angry exchange between Lillith and Heather. Cinny was disconcerted. "This is unbelievable! Are you saying that Heather thinks the famous Lillith has made porn movies?"

Tess could imagine the story on the front page of *The National Scoop.* The Hansels would be mortified. The media hounds would camp outside their house. Lillith would probably have to go into hiding. "Maybe Heather is wrong," Tess said hopefully.

"I know how we could find out," Cinny said eagerly. "Let's watch the tape."

"We can't open Heather's mail! I believe that's a federal offense."

"Come on, Tess. Who will know? Just make that tear a little longer, and the tape will slide right out. You can tell Heather it was torn when you got it. That's not a lie."

"We shouldn't," Tess said.

Cinny merely looked at her.

Tess knew she could not be in the same house with that tape for very long before her curiosity overcame her judgment. She gave up the argument. "Oh, why not," she said and proceeded to lengthen the tear enough to extract the tape.

"After all," Cinny said, "Heather could be wrong about Lillith. You really need to be sure, one way or the other."

"Certainly." Tess was far too eager to know the truth to listen to the niggling little voice of her conscience. They went into the sitting room and Tess inserted the tape in the VCR. They settled on the sofa to watch.

Tess had never seen blatant porn before, and it was a little embarrassing to be seeing it for the first time with her cousin. *Barbie's Playhouse* started with a roguishly handsome man, wearing pants so tight he must have been poured into them, knocking on a door. The door was opened by a bleached-blond woman wearing a black negligee. He asked for Barbie, and she smiled coyly and invited him in.

After a brief, inane conversation full of double entendres, they went to the bedroom where Barbie did a striptease for him. The woman had a nice body, but Tess was more interested in her face, which she'd been studying since she first came on screen. The resemblance to Lillith was undeniable. She was much younger and her hair was bleached platinum, but the famous face was recognizable, down to the tiny mole on the left side of her mouth. It couldn't be anybody else.

As the couple on the screen fell on the bed in a tangle of naked arms, legs, and torsos, Cinny said, "The storyline's a bit thin, isn't it?"

"What storyline?" Tess muttered. "Cinny, I'd hate for anybody to catch us watching this." She reached for the remote.

Cinny grabbed her hand. "Wait a minute. I want to get another good look at her face."

"I've seen enough," Tess sighed as she picked up the book lying on the coffee table. It was the Dr. Patrice Singleton bestseller, the one Heather had left in the apartment. Tess opened it and scanned the front cover flap, while Cinny leaned forward to stare at the screen. The only sound coming from the video was a series of sighs and grunts. Tess flipped to the back cover flap and read the author blurb. Dr. Patrice had received her bachelors and masters degrees from the University of Kansas and her Ph.D. from Columbia.

"OK," Cinny said. "It's Lillith, all right. She could dye her hair purple, but that face gives her away."

Tess was now staring at the photograph of Dr. Patrice. "What did you say?"

Cinny reached for the remote and stopped the tape, then punched the rewind button. "I said it's Lillith. You can't disguise your face unless you get plastic surgery—or wear a mask or . . ."

"Or glasses," Tess murmured, still staring at Dr. Patrice.

"Yeah, that might have helped, but she wouldn't wear

glasses while playing a sex goddess, would she?"

Tess only half heard what Cinny was saying. Her thoughts were on Dr. Patrice, who had attended the University of Kansas. Pat Snell, who'd dyed her hair and wore eyeglasses with plain glass lenses, claimed to be from Topeka, which she would probably be familiar with if she'd spent several years in Kansas.

Was it possible . . . ?

Cinny got up, ejected the rewound tape, and stuffed it back in the mailer. Then she stood, looking down at Tess. "What are you looking at?"

"Nothing." Tess closed the book. "I—well, I think it's despicable of Heather to want to expose Lillith's foray into x-rated movies. Lillith looked like a teenager in that movie. She made it years ago, and she's managed to put that part of her life behind her. I'm sure she's tried her best to forget she ever did anything so stupid. Now she's retired from modeling, married, and working at being a wife and mother, and Heather wants to toss a bomb into the middle of the decent life Lillith has made for herself."

"Yeah, it's probably the worst thing anybody could do to Lillith," Cinny agreed.

An image of Lillith wielding the dumbbell to destroy Heather's camera flashed into Tess's mind, possibly the same dumbbell that had been used to murder Marcia Yoder.

"You know, Tess, " Cinny was saying, "if you don't give the tape to Heather, maybe she won't do the story."

Tess pushed the image of Lillith from her mind and thought about Heather. Would she forget doing the story on Lillith if Tess didn't give her the video? Tess doubted it. She didn't think Heather, the relentless reporter, could be derailed that easily.

The image of Lillith bringing the dumbbell down with all her strength returned to Tess. In addition to giving Heather Brackland a juicy story for the tabloid, the evidence on the tape gave Lillith a very strong motive for wanting to shut Heather up for good.

People *could* be pushed beyond their ability to control

their actions, Tess mused. Everybody had a breaking point.

"Poor Lillith," Cinny murmured. "That Heather Brackland is a piece of work. Imagine having a job where you dig up dirt on famous people and then spread it all over that disgusting tabloid."

The revelation about Heather's previous career and the one of Rudy's financial troubles were about to hit the Hansels at the same time, if Heather had her way. Rudy and Lillith were in for a rough go. "I don't want to give the tape to Heather," Tess said unhappily, "but I don't want to give it to Chief Butts, either."

"Then don't," Cinny advised. "Things get lost in the mail all the time, right?"

As if Tess's words had conjured him up, there was a rapid pounding on her door and Butts yelled loudly enough to be heard throughout the neighborhood, "Tess! Open up! We're here with a warrant!"

Cinny's blue eyes darted to the door, then back to Tess's face, her expression horrified. "My God, he's going to arrest somebody!"

"No, I think he's here to search the house."

Tess opened the door. Officer Struthers waited in the foyer while an impatient Butts stepped into the apartment and thrust a piece of paper under Tess's nose. The search warrant.

"We'll want to look everywhere," Butts announced. "We'll finish up in here. I'll need your keys, in case your guests aren't in their rooms."

"Wait a minute," Tess protested. "Are you saying you mean to search my apartment, too?"

"Have to be thorough, Tess."

Tess was outraged. "You surely can't suspect me!"

"Nobody is above suspicion," Butts said sanctimoniously. He peered at her through his eyeglasses, looking quite satisfied with himself. He was doing this to aggravate her, Tess suspected, and she would simply have to grin and bear it.

She went to her office, took a minute to get her temper in check, then got the master key for Butts. "If I'm not here when you finish, please leave the key on my desk."

Butts stomped out of the apartment, handed the master key to Struthers, then went into the guest parlor where Lida and Cail were conducting a discussion group.

"Everybody stay where you are," Butts blared. "Just go on with what you're doing."

Meanwhile, Officer Struthers bounded up the stairs to begin searching the guest rooms.

Tess ventured into the parlor and saw Butts plowing through the dining room and entering the kitchen. "Howdy, Miz Bogart," he said to Gertie. "Can you show me where you keep your rat poison?"

Gertie started explaining that they didn't have any rat poison, but Butts ignored her and began pulling out drawers and opening cabinet doors, rummaging through the contents.

In the parlor, Lillith croaked, "Rat poison, what in the world—? What's this all about, Tess?"

Tess shrugged helplessly. "All I can tell you is he's got a search warrant," she said shortly.

Cinny, who'd followed Tess out of the apartment, said, "What's rat poison got to do with anything?"

"Don't ask me," Tess said curtly, though it obviously had something to do with Heather's sudden illness. She turned and went back to her sitting room.

Cinny followed. "Tess, there's something you're not telling me."

Instead of responding to Cinny's accusation, Tess said, "I don't want to be around when they go through my apartment," Tess said. "Let's get out of here." She glanced at the mailer containing the videotape, then picked it up and took it with her.

Chapter 24

As Cinny and Tess headed down the front walk, they saw Lida's van peeling out of the guest parking area next door.

Tess watched the van whiz down the street, breaking the speed limit by at least twenty miles. "That's Lida's van. Where do you suppose she's going?"

"Wherever it is, she's in a big hurry to get there," Cinny said.

"The fitness center probably."

"Do you suppose Butts knows she left?"

Butts had told the guests to stay in the parlor, but if Lida had left by the front door, it was possible Butts hadn't seen her go. "Let's follow her," Tess said. "We'll take your car. She'd recognize mine."

Cinny started her Thunderbird and sped away from Iris House. Two right turns later, they caught sight of the back of Lida's van. The van's windows were tinted, so it was impossible to tell if the driver was alone.

Hanging back about a block, Cinny followed the van through the business district and continued several blocks south. She grinned at Tess. "This is lots more fun than selling books!"

Fun was not the word Tess would have used. If

Lida recognized them, how would she explain their following her?

It soon became clear that Tess's assumption was correct. The van was headed to the fitness center. When it turned in behind the center, Cinny drove on past and parked at the curb where they could see the van.

The driver's door opened and Cail jumped out. He ran up the backstairs leading to his apartment. As he unlocked the door, he darted a glance over his shoulder and Tess got a good look at his face. The man was scared.

"If only we could see what he's doing in there," Cinny said.

"I wonder if he's packing," Tess murmured. Cail had certainly looked frightened enough to run away.

But a few minutes later, Cail emerged on the landing at the top of the stairs with nothing but a small sack in one hand. He ran down the stairs toward the van. Instead of getting in the van, he hesitated beside the center's trash barrel, then ran to a barrel behind another business half a block away. He lifted the lid and threw in the sack. Returning to the van, he drove away. Cinny turned her head and Tess ducked out of sight until he had driven past. At the corner, he turned back toward town.

"Should we keep following him?" Cinny asked.

"No, I think he's headed back to Iris House. I want to see what he put in that trash barrel. I'm willing to bet it's some kind of pesticide."

"Really?" Cinny asked as she got out to follow Tess up the alley to the trash barrel. Tess lifted the lid to retrieve the sack Cail had removed from his apartment. It had settled atop a stack of newspapers. Tess lifted it out and read the label: *Rodent Poison—Keep Out of Reach of Children.*

"Did you bring your cellular phone?" Tess asked Cinny.

"It's in my purse."

"Good." Tess returned the sack to the trash barrel.

Back at the car, Cinny said, "Tess, what's going on? Why are the police looking for rat poison?"

Since Butts had told her not to tell anyone that Heather had been poisoned, Tess said, "I'm not privy to Chief Butts's thoughts." She used Cinny's phone to call Iris House and ask for Chief Butts.

After a few moment's wait, Butts barked, "Yes!"

Tess told him what they had observed and where he could find the poison.

"Damn!" Butts growled. "We were going to the fitness center when we left here. Should've gone there first." He hung up without another word. No thanks. No goodbye. It was vintage Butts.

Tess had meant to ask when they would be finished searching her apartment, but Butts hadn't given her a chance. She decided to go to the bookshop. Cinny could drive her home after a while.

When Cinny dropped her off at Iris House two hours later, it was late afternoon. Tess saw that Lida's van was parked beside Tess's car in the paved area next to the fence which marked the north boundary of the large lawn.

When Tess entered the foyer, she saw Lida sitting alone in the guest parlor, her head bowed. None of the guests was in sight, nor was Cail. Lida didn't appear to have heard Tess come in. She could be asleep, or she could be praying.

It was almost six o'clock, the time Lida usually picked up the guests for dinner in town. Always before, she'd gone home to change clothes before returning for them, but she still wore the same exercise clothes she'd worn all day. The last shafts of the day's sunlight glittered on the glass base of the lamp beside Lida's chair.

Tess hesitated in the doorway. "Lida?"

Slowly she lifted her head to look at Tess, a searching and bewildered look. "They've taken Cail in for questioning." She sucked in a shaky breath. "I don't understand what's going on, Tess."

Tess wasn't about to tell her. Instead she mouthed an insincere platitude. "I'm sure it's just routine. They'll probably question everybody again."

But Lida wasn't buying it. "While the police were here, Cail went back to his apartment. He said he'd forgotten his wallet. When he got back, Chief Butts met him in the foyer and said he wanted Cail to go down to the station with him. Cail asked why, and Butts just said something had come up that they needed to talk to Cail about."

Tess's response was a noncommittal "Hmmm."

"Why were they asking Gertie about rat poison?"

"Perhaps Gertie knows," Tess said, thinking that Lida must surely realize any minute that she was obviously being unforthcoming.

"Gertie's gone home," Lida went on. "I don't think they found any poison here. After Cail and Chief Butts left, Officer Struthers showed me a search warrant for the fitness center." Lida shook her head helplessly. "I gave him the key and told him to leave it in the mailbox when he left. I couldn't face going down there and standing around while they searched. I told him we'd had a mouse problem last year, in the apartment as well as the center, and they'd probably find what was left of the poison at the center somewhere."

"You can't remember where you put it?"

She shook her head. "I haven't needed it in months. Maybe I threw it away. I just can't remember."

"Try not to worry, Lida."

She nodded. "I told Cail to meet us at the restaurant if Butts lets him go in time. I'm sure there's a simple explanation for all this." She sounded less than convinced.

A very simple explanation indeed, Tess thought. It would seem that Butts was working up to arresting Cail for murder.

The telephone rang and Tess answered in the kitchen. It was Cail wanting to talk to Lida. Tess handed her the phone.

"Cail, where are you?" Lida asked. "What? You can't be serious. All right. I'll take care of it." She hung up and turned to Tess. "They're keeping him overnight. Can they do that?"

"I expect so."

"They haven't arrested him yet, but why would they keep him there unless—" Lida couldn't bring herself to voice the terrible thought.

"Oh, Lida, I'm sorry."

She looked frantically around the room, as if trying to remember where she'd left something valuable. "I— I have to find a lawyer, but who? Oh, I know, I'll call the one who handled my purchase of the center. If he doesn't do this kind of thing, he should be able to tell me who does. Cail says he's not saying another word to the police without a lawyer." She reached for the phone, then turned back to Tess. "Could you possibly see that my people get dinner? I'll reimburse you later."

"I can't get that many people in my car," Tess said.

"You could make two trips or—oh, God, I don't know. I can't think straight, Tess."

Lida was on the verge of tears. "I'll figure out something," Tess said. "There's a deli about a mile down the road. Perhaps we could walk."

"They can have a sandwich and salad," Lida said. "Nonfat dressing, no mayonnaise." She lifted the receiver and began to dial.

The guests were none too happy about being fobbed off with a sandwich and salad for dinner, not to mention having to walk a mile to get it. As Rudy put it, "It's insulting, after what we paid to come to this damned retreat."

They had pulled two of the deli's tables together and were waiting for their sandwiches. "Lida had an unexpected emergency," Tess said. "It couldn't be helped."

"I saw Chief Butts leaving Iris House with Cail," Pat Snell said. "What's that all about?"

"I don't know," Tess told her. Every time Pat's attention had been focused elsewhere since they sat down, Tess had studied her face. Was it the same face as the one in the photograph in Dr. Patrice's book? There were definitely similarities, though Pat's face didn't look as narrow as Dr. Patrice's—but, then, she'd come to the retreat to lose weight.

If Pat really was Dr. Patrice, it was understandable why she'd been so adamant about not having her picture taken.

"Tess?"

She hadn't been aware that Pat was talking to her.

"I'm sorry, Pat. What did you say?"

"You're so quiet, like your mind is miles away. Did the police find something at Iris House, something to do with Marcia's murder?"

"There was nothing to find," Tess said. "Nothing I know of, anyway."

"They didn't take anything with them," Pat said, "except Cail, of course. So they evidently didn't find whatever it was they were looking for."

"Do you suppose they've arrested Cail for Marcia's murder?" Dorinda pondered.

"Could be," Pat responded. "Lida seemed awfully upset about the whole thing. And I think she's not with us now because she couldn't face the questions about Cail. It's obvious she's crazy about him."

"Lord knows why," Dorinda murmured, then after a moment added, "In a way it would be a relief just to know who killed my sister."

"Well," Lillith said, "if there had been any evidence against anybody at Iris House, they'd have found it, the way they went through that place—like a cyclone. They left the suite in a big mess."

Tess's apartment had been thoroughly ransacked, too. In the bedroom, they'd left clothes from the dresser drawers strewn about. She would have to put the apartment to rights before she could go to bed.

"Yeah, they even stripped the sheets off my bed," Kent grumbled. "Now I have to put them back on before I can go to sleep. I don't even know how to make a bed."

"It's about time you learned," Lillith said.

He scowled at her, and Rudy said, "She's right, son. We can't expect Lillith to do everything for us."

"Mom did," Kent muttered.

Tess saw the flash of irritation in Lillith's eyes before she pressed her lips together, as if to keep from lashing out at Kent.

Their sandwiches arrived and Tess watched Lillith nibble daintily at hers, as though she had little appetite. Tess felt a rush of sympathy for her. Kent obviously resented her for marrying his father, and clearly hadn't wanted to come to the retreat. In fact, Tess had heard Kent tell his father that Lillith had tricked them into coming. There was enough stress in that family situation without sensational tabloid stories adding to it.

She tried to distract Kent. "Kent, I think you've lost weight already."

He brightened. "Really? Today I ran almost a mile before I had to stop and walk. Lida said I had the makings of a runner if I lose twenty-five pounds. Do you think she's right?"

"I can't see why not."

"I may go out for track next year," Kent said hesitantly.

"I'll run with you in the evenings," Lillith offered. "We can make out a schedule, set goals for ourselves. There are several 5K runs in our area that we could enter, once we've trained a while. You can be in great shape by next fall."

"Maybe," Kent said doubtfully. He was clearly having trouble seeing himself running races.

"We might even get your father to join us," Lillith went on.

"Would you, Dad?" Kent asked.

Rudy looked alarmed and mumbled, "We'll see."

Ignoring the desultory conversation that continued around her, Tess ate her sandwich in silence and wondered what was going on at the police station. Was the rat poison enough evidence for Chief Butts to arrest Cail? Tess didn't know, but it seemed circumstantial at best, and Cail was too cool a customer to be badgered into confessing.

Chapter 25

Cail sat, arms folded, his chair tipped back on two legs, refusing to answer Butts's questions, except to say "No comment" to everything. The rest of the time, he was looking around the bare-walled room like he was on holiday, enjoying the sights. Rarely had Butts questioned such a calm and collected suspect.

Butts was steaming, and now the tattered threads of patience he'd been holding on to for the last hour deserted him completely. "Look, scuzbag, you killed that woman and poisoned Heather Brackland."

Cail managed to look surprised. "Heather was poisoned?"

"Damned straight. You know it and I know it. We've got a witness who says you paid him to threaten Brackland, and you were seen getting rid of evidence before we conducted a search of your apartment."

A small smile twisted Cail's lips. "No comment."

Butts wheeled, ripped open the door, and stormed out of the interrogation room, slamming the door behind him. As he walked away, Cail yelled through the closed door, "Nice talking to you, too, Chief!"

Butts halted, his fists balled, tempted to go back

and have another go at it. But better judgment prevailed. If he didn't get away from Cail Hurst, he was going to lose it completely and punch the weasel's smug face. And if he ever touched the man, he wasn't sure he could stop. Then he'd be up on brutality charges and Hurst would walk.

He had tracked down Chuck Bowers at the Red Dog and got him to admit that Hurst paid him to call Heather Brackland and threaten her. But when he'd sprung that on Hurst at the beginning of the interrogation, the man had shown absolutely no reaction. Butts had then hit him with the fact that two witnesses saw him get rid of the poison. Hurst had offered a feeble excuse. And then he'd refused to say anything more without his lawyer present.

An hour ago, Hurst had called Lida Darnell and told her to find him an attorney. Meantime, Butts had put in a call to the D.A., laid out what he had on Hurst, and had been told in no uncertain terms it wasn't enough to make an arrest.

Dammit, his stomach felt like he'd swallowed a cactus. He rummaged around in his desk until he found an old roll of antacids and swallowed two tablets. Then he poured a glass of milk from the carton in the portable fridge in his office and sagged into his chair, exhausted.

He stared glumly out the window at the night-shrouded street. This case was driving him crazy. One murder and one attempted murder, and he had the murderer in custody but couldn't arrest him.

Well, he wasn't letting Hurst go. If he had to, he'd turn him over to the California authorities and hold him until they got there. Damned D.A. would probably tell him he couldn't keep Hurst in custody that long, so he wasn't even going to ask.

He gulped some milk and made a face. He hated milk, but the way his stomach felt, he didn't dare drink any more coffee today. The doc had said he had a peptic ulcer and he should stop the coffee altogether. He was down to two or three cups a day, but damned if he could give it up completely.

At one point, he'd told Hurst he was going to arrest

him, but Muscle Man had just sneered at him. He'd probably had dealings with law enforcement before and figured Butts would have already read him his rights if he had enough evidence to make an arrest.

Butts hadn't yet mentioned the California charges. He was keeping that in reserve as Plan B. He'd spring it on Hurst at the last minute if it came to that.

Okay, what *did* he have?

Heather Brackland was threatening to turn Hurst in to the L.A. cops if he didn't come up with the money she claimed he owed her. Early on, when he'd still been responding to questions, Hurst had told Butts that he didn't owe Brackland a dime and wasn't going to pay. That and his weak explanation as to why he'd tossed the poison was all he'd said before he started replying "No comment" to everything Butts said. Of course, Hurst didn't know that Butts knew about the blackmail and what Heather was holding over his head.

The blackmail gave Butts the motive for murder.

As to the poison, Hurst claimed he'd heard Butts ask Gertie Bogart about rat poison and knew immediately that they must have found poison in Brackland's tests. He figured he had to be the prime suspect, since he was the only one in Victoria Springs who'd known Heather longer than a few days. When he heard Butts mention poison, he'd remembered the rat poison, which he'd taken from the center and spread around after he saw a mouse in his apartment. He'd panicked and gone back to his apartment to get rid of the poison, which he now regretted, or so he said, because it made him look guilty when he was as pure as the driven snow. That was Hurst's story and he was sticking to it.

Those two dingbat women had had no better sense than to follow Hurst and watch him dispose of the poison. And the bartender at the Red Dog had told Butts that a young woman fitting Tess's description, and accompanied by another young woman, had come to the saloon asking questions about Cail. One of these days Tess Darcy was going to go too far to "help" the police and get herself in real hot water.

This time, however, he was glad she'd followed Hurst, even though he'd chewed her out for it when she reported it to him. Now the D.A. was saying it wasn't enough.

That was it, then. He had motive, he had the threatening phone call, and he had the rat poison Hurst had trashed. All circumstantial, and not enough to make the D.A. schedule an arraignment.

One thing he hadn't admitted to the D.A. Even though he was sure he had the murderer in custody, something kept nagging at Butts. Hurst had Chuck Bowers threaten Heather, telling her to leave town, then went immediately to Iris House and killed the woman he thought was Heather. Anybody with a grain of sense would have waited a day or two to see if the threat was going to work before he committed murder.

Butts couldn't come up with a logical explanation for that—unless Hurst had been too drunk to think straight. Which was a distinct possibility, as the Red Dog bartender said Hurst had had several beers before he left the bar the night of the murder. And he'd taken a six-pack with him.

The phone rang and his hand jerked, almost spilling his milk. He set the glass down and grabbed the receiver. "Butts here."

"Chief, this is John Finerty. I've been retained to represent Cail Marrs. What are the charges against him?"

"Hurst," Butts barked.

"Pardon me?"

"His name's Cail Hurst. Marrs is an alias."

Clearly surprised by this bit of information, Finerty paused, then demanded, "Has he admitted to that?"

"He ain't admitted anything. He won't talk, but your client, Cail *Hurst*, is wanted on drug dealing charges in L.A. Now, he's murdered one woman and attempted to kill another."

"You're throwing around a lot of charges here, Chief. I assume you have the evidence to back them up."

Cornered, Butts made a snap decision. "I'm still working on the murder charge. In the meantime, I'm holding

him for the California authorities." He slammed down
the phone.

After muttering a few well-chosen oaths, he picked
up the receiver again, dialed information, and got the
number for the LAPD.

Chapter 26

After returning to Iris House, Tess closeted herself in her apartment, called the police station, and asked for Chief Butts.

"Butts here."

"Chief, this is Tess Darcy. Lida is very upset about you taking Cail in for questioning. Is he under arrest for Marcia's murder?"

"Hell, no! Damned D.A. says we don't have enough evidence, so I'm extraditing him to California. They're gonna send somebody out to get him tomorrow. He was dealing drugs out there. Probably doing it here, too."

"Oh. Well, that's not going to please Lida, but at least he's not been arrested on a murder charge."

"I know he did it," Butts snarled, "and he knows I know he did it. I haven't given up on putting a case together yet."

"You're absolutely sure he's the killer?"

"Without a doubt."

"Thanks, Chief. I'll let you get back to work."

Tess hung up. At least Cail was in custody. She'd better call the hospital and tell Heather she could come out of hiding now.

Heather was vastly relieved when Tess gave her the news. The doctor was releasing her tomorrow, and she asked Tess if she could pick her up and take her back to Iris House. With Cail out of the way, she might as well stay till the retreat was over. It had cost too much not to finish.

Fortunately, Tess hadn't gotten around to packing Heather's clothes yet, so Heather could pick up her computer, camera, and printouts and go right back to irritating the other guests.

As Tess was about to ring off, Heather asked, "Has any mail come for me?"

Evidently she was expecting the videotape. Tess's gaze fell on the mailer containing the tape, which she'd laid on the coffee table when she returned from Cinny's bookstore that afternoon, and with hardly a qualm, she decided to lie. "Sorry, no," she said and made an excuse to end the conversation.

What should she do with the tape? Give it to Lillith? Turn it over to Heather? Give it to the police? She'd have to decide before she picked up Heather tomorrow.

Dr. Patrice's book lay beside the videotape. With Pat Snell's image from dinner fresh in her memory, Tess picked up the book to study the author's photograph. According to the information about the author, Dr. Patrice lived in Chicago, where her show was syndicated by a radio station there. The station's call letters were included.

Tess tried information for Patrice Singleton's phone number and was told it was unlisted. But she'd expected that. Well-known people had to get unlisted numbers to keep from having their lives constantly interrupted by fans and crazies. Tess had heard Dr. Patrice's program a couple of times, and she tended to be pretty combative with callers. One of them might take enough umbrage at the treatment to decide to harm her, which had actually happened to another radio personality recently. Hence the unlisted number.

Before she could get the information operator again, to ask for the number of the radio station where Dr. Patrice worked, Luke phoned.

"Sidney and I have an eight o'clock conference call with one of our clients," he said. "He's nervous about the drop in the market, and we have to calm him down.

Some people want to sell everything just when a good buying opportunity presents itself."

"I understand," Tess told him. "I know I'd be too emotionally involved to ever buy and sell stocks on my own. Fortunately for me, I'm marrying a man who can handle all that for the both of us."

"Absolutely. Now, sweetheart, since I can't leave, why don't you come here for the night? We could go out for a late dinner after the conference call."

"I've just had dinner," Tess said, then filled him in on what had happened that day.

"Well, that's a relief. With Cail Marrs in custody, you'll be safe there. I'd still like you to come here, of course."

"Thanks, sweetheart, but I'm really bushed. I think I'll make it an early night."

Luke agreed reluctantly. When he hung up, Tess got the number for the Chicago radio station and dialed. She told the woman who answered that she needed to speak to Patrice Singleton. She knew the doctor probably wasn't at the station at the moment, she said, but could she leave a number with a message for Dr. Patrice to call her back?

She was informed that "Dr. Patrice is on a three-month sabbatical and can't be reached."

Tess hung up and had another look at the photograph in the book. She was almost certain now that the woman in the photograph and Pat Snell were one and the same. After studying Pat's face at the restaurant, she could see similarities that had escaped her before.

She laid the book aside, then left the apartment and went up the stairs to the Annabel Jane Room.

When Pat opened the door, she wasn't wearing her glasses, and Tess's last lingering doubts were removed.

"May I come in?"

Pat hesitated before she said, "Sure. What's up?"

Tess sat down in the chair by the window while Pat found her glasses and put them on, probably castigating herself for forgetting and opening the door without them.

"There's something I think you should know," Tess said.

Frowning, Pat sat stiffly on the end of the bed. "Is Cail Marrs under arrest?"

"Yes. He's being sent to California to face some outstanding charges there."

"My God! You mean he's killed before?"

"The California charges have to do with dealing drugs."

"Oh. So they still don't know who killed Marcia?"

"Chief Butts is sure Cail did it. He's just not ready to file a murder charge yet."

"I see," Pat said reflectively. "Well, at least he's out of the way. So, is that what you wanted to tell me?"

"That and—well, Pat, I have reason to believe that somebody has been checking into your background. Apparently you don't manage a craft mall—you don't even live in Topeka."

Anger flashed in her eyes. "You checked up on me?"

"I can't afford to lose a week's room rent." Pat had paid cash for the first week when she checked in.

"You'll get paid!" she snapped. "I'll pay you now, in fact." She got up and went for her purse. "Here." She opened her wallet and extracted a fistful of hundred-dollar bills. She counted out enough for her second week's stay at Iris House and thrust them at Tess. Obviously she'd come prepared to pay for everything in cash, as a check or credit card would reveal her true identity.

"Thank you," Tess said, "but there's something else you should know. I'm afraid your true identity is about to come out."

Pat stared at her open-mouthed. "Oh, my God!" She fell back on the bed as if she'd been shoved. Before Tess could get up to see if she was all right, however, she shot to her feet, jerked her glasses off, and threw them on the bed. "I've been so careful. The people at the radio station don't even know where I am. This can't be happening!"

Tess fixed a puzzled expression on her face. "I don't

understand why you're using a false name, anyway. What difference does it make if people here know you're really Dr. Patrice Singleton?"

Pat advanced toward Tess's chair. "Who told you that? It was Heather, wasn't it?"

Tess met her gaze without flinching, though it wasn't easy. Pat was furious. "No. I figured it out for myself. Your photograph in the book Lida is having everybody read gave you away."

"Who else knows?" she demanded.

"Nobody—yet. And I don't plan to tell anyone. But, Pat, if I figured it out, don't you think Heather will? You were so adamant about not having your picture taken, you made her suspicious. She had the researchers at the tabloid check Kansas records for your name. They didn't find it."

"I knew it! Thank God she's not coming back here."

"Oh, but she is. Now that Cail's in jail, she decided to finish out the retreat."

Pat threw out both arms. "Well, this is just great. Heather is going to keep on till she knows the truth. Before she went to the hospital, she kept saying I looked familiar. The woman's relentless." Pat ran both hands through her short, black hair. "And then that ditsy Marcia had to point out that my hair was dyed."

Tess thought everybody had already figured that one out before Marcia commented on it. The color was *too* black to be natural. She watched Pat walk to the window and stare out. Pat let her forehead drop until it touched the glass for a moment, then she turned around. "Why did I have to choose the same weight-loss program as Heather Brackland? Why didn't I ask for the names of the other registrants before I signed up?" Abruptly, she slumped down on the bed. "*That woman* is going to destroy my career."

"Oh, Pat, surely you're exaggerating. Even if she decides to do a story on you, how can that destroy your career?"

"Don't be dense," Pat snapped. "If it comes out that I have a weight problem, my credibility as a nutrition

and fitness authority will be ruined. I'm going on tour
with my new book in June. I was counting on that to
help boost my show ratings, which have slumped the
past few months. I have to lose thirty pounds by then,
but what good will it do if that filthy tabloid tells the
world I've just spent three months shucking the weight?"
She jumped up again and made a restless circle of the
room.

Tess could see how an article in a national tabloid
about Pat's weight-loss efforts might cause problems for
Pat, but agreeing with the woman's doomsaying would
only unnerve her further. Tess tried to sound encouraging. "There's another way to look at all this."

Pat, who'd stopped pacing to brace herself with both
hands against the closed door, straightened up and
snorted. "Oh, really? Pray tell, how I can possibly salvage my career if this comes out?"

"Suppose you go on the radio and tell your listeners
that you can empathize with them because you've had
a struggle with weight yourself. You can offer them the
support of somebody who's been there."

Pat threw up her hands in despair. "Oh, please—"

"No, think about it. Before you go on tour, you can
do a whole program, telling them how you lost the
weight and how you plan to keep it off. Knowing what
you've gone through should be an inspiration for them."
Tess hestitated, then added, "I've heard your program,
Pat, and, frankly, you come across as arrogant and con-
descending. You might appeal to a wider audience if you
were more sympathetic. That would help your ratings."

Pat snorted. "Gosh, Tess, don't hold back. Tell me
what you really think." She walked over to the bed,
flopped down on her back, and stared up at the ceiling.

"I'm merely suggesting that you become a more com-
passionate listener."

"You don't get it, Tess. That's the image I project—
no nonsense, no excuses."

"Then change your image."

She was silent for a few moments. "Admitting that I

have a weight problem is just too risky, Tess, after some of the things I've said on the air . . ."

"Honestly," said Tess, "I think that may be your only viable option—if Heather writes her story. And she's coming back here tomorrow."

Pat groaned, sounding as if she were in pain. "Damn the woman! She's going to keep badgering me about where she's seen me before. Truthfully, Tess, I could cheerfully kill her."

Pat was in such distress that Tess thought she probably didn't realize the implications of what she'd said. Had she already tried to kill Heather? Tess didn't want to give space to that thought. Butts was sure he had the murderer in custody, and he was still working on getting more evidence in the case against him. And Cail had certainly reacted like a guilty person when he got rid of the rat poison.

The murderer had to be Cail. If Cail wasn't guilty, then the killer was still a guest at Iris House.

Chapter 27

The next morning, as soon as Lida and the guests returned from their morning run, Lida knocked on Tess's door.

Tess left a cinnamon roll and coffee on her kitchen table and went to answer. "Good morning, Lida," Tess said, though Lida looked as though she'd had many better mornings than this one.

"May I come in for a minute?"

"Of course." Tess went to the coffee table and picked up Dr. Patrice's book. She handed it to Lida. "I've been meaning to give this to you. Heather left it here before she went into the hospital."

Lida took the book and sat down in Primrose's favorite chair, as the cat had streaked out of the sitting room when Lida's knock sounded at the door. "I'll return the book to Heather," she said. "I'm glad she decided to finish out the retreat."

"I hope she doesn't cause you any more trouble."

Lida shrugged. "I was probably too defensive with her. She told me *Cail* was the liar, that he was not what he seemed to be, that I didn't really know him. I thought she was making it all up because he walked out on her. Now . . . well, I'm not sure what to believe. I stopped to tell you something I just learned. Cail is going to be sent back to California to face drug charges."

180

"I gathered as much, from something Chief Butts said."

"I called Chief Butts early this morning. I was going to demand that he release Cail from jail." She made a self-mocking sound. "But before I could finish my tirade, Butts told me about the California charges and said he wouldn't be a bit surprised if Cail was selling steroids and amphetamines to some of the customers at my gym. That's what he was doing in L.A.—pushing steroids to men who wanted to muscle up and amphetamines to anybody who wanted to lose weight quickly." She drew in a shuddering breath. "If he'd been caught pushing drugs at my place of business, I could have been implicated."

"There's no evidence he dealt drugs here, Lida."

"Oh, he admitted it to me. I spoke to Cail after I talked to Chief Butts. He said he'd sold steroids a few times, but not at the gym. He also swore that he didn't kill Marcia or poison anybody. Chief Butts is sure he did both. It seems Heather was given arsenic, which explains all that searching for rat poison."

Evidently Butts no longer thought it necessary to keep Heather's poisoning a secret.

"I'm sorry, Lida. I know you depended on Cail a lot."

"Too much," Lida admitted. "I can't believe I was about ready to give him a share of my business."

"You're lucky you found out the truth in time."

She sighed. "That's the bright side of this, if there is a bright side." Her voice wobbled and she stopped to swallow tears. "Two days ago," Lida went on, "I would have laughed in the Chief's face if he'd accused Cail of one murder and one attempted murder. But I'm not laughing now. Butts said Cail went back to the gym yesterday to get rid of the rat poison we had there. Butts says that's where he got the poison for Heather." Her voice broke again. "I loved him so much, Tess."

"You loved the man you thought he was, Lida."

"Yes, that's true." She tried to laugh, but it came out a hurt little whimper. "I should have known he wasn't in love with me, a woman fourteen years his senior. He was using me, just like he used Heather, and Lord knows how many other women. But I couldn't think straight. There's no fool like an old fool, as they say."

"Or like a woman in love," Tess murmured.

Lida smiled through tears. "I've been on my own for a long time. I've learned to be tough. I still have my business, and I'll get over Cail. I'll find another trainer."

"I know you will."

Lida stood, hugging the book to her chest. "I'll go have my breakfast now. I just wanted you to know what was going on with Cail."

"I meant to thank you for encouraging Kent Hansel about his running," Tess blurted out, in an attempt to boost Lida's spirits. "He's actually talking about going out for track next school year. Lillith is going to help him train."

She smiled weakly. "I'm glad to hear that. Now, if Lillith can only get Rudy on some kind of fitness program."

When Lida was gone, Tess went back to her breakfast. As she ate, she watched the men working on the new addition from her kitchen window. The framework for the walls was up, and she could now get an idea of what Iris House would look like when the construction was finished—wonderful.

Watching the new rooms take shape made her more eager than ever for June to arrive. She hadn't picked out paint and wallpaper yet, as Wayne Armory had reminded her yesterday. She had to carve out several hours next week to make the selections, a project she looked forward to, or would have, if she didn't have so much else on her mind. She must decide on window treatments, too, and find somebody to create and install them.

If only she had a houseful of ordinary tourist guests, so that she could apply all her mind to preparing a home for her and Luke. But she would have the current irascible crew for another week yet.

She pulled her gaze and thoughts away from the construction going on outside and forced herself to think about the *Barbie's Playhouse* videotape. She must decide what to do with it before she picked up Heather that afternoon.

If she gave it to Heather, she would be handing the woman the evidence she needed to write an exposé of Lillith. Not that Heather wouldn't do it anyway, but Tess hated to aid and abet such unsavory business.

She could, of course, destroy and dispose of the tape and claim she never received it. In which case, Heather would likely send for another copy.

She could not think of any action on her part that would guarantee Heather would change her mind about writing the story.

Which left only the option of forewarning Lillith. At least then, the Hansels could brace themselves for the onslaught of publicity when *The National Scoop* ran the story. It was her only option really; she didn't think she could live with herself if she handed over the tape to Heather and left Lillith in ignorance until the tabloid story broke. She would decide later whether she should inform Chief Butts. He was certain he had the murderer, and handing him a motive for another suspect would only cloud the issue. She was sure Butts would not appreciate that.

There was one small problem, though. Tess was not fully convinced Butts had the murderer. Oh, Cail had had motive and opportunity, and he'd tried to get rid of evidence. He had engaged in criminal activity in the past, and he was certainly the person Tess *hoped* had done the deed, but a niggling little doubt would not leave her alone.

Other people had strong motives for wanting Heather dead, as strong as Cail's. It would surely simplify things, and ease Tess's mind, if the man confessed. Which was as likely to happen as a Missouri ice storm in July.

One problem at a time, she told herself.

Her chance to talk to Lillith alone came during the morning break. As the other guests were heading upstairs to read the assigned chapters in Dr. Patrice's book, Rudy and Kent Hansel went outside, books in hand. The temperature was hovering near seventy-five today and the pair had evidently decided to do their reading in the garden.

As soon as the front door closed behind Rudy and Kent, Tess called to Lillith, who'd reached the top of the stairs. "Lillith, could I see you for a minute?"

Lillith came back down, a questioning look on her face, and followed Tess into her apartment. Dispensing with preliminaries, Tess drew the videotape from the mailer and handed it to Lillith. "This came for Heather. She'll be back here this afternoon, but I decided to give the tape to you and let Heather think it got lost in the mail."

Tess expected shock, tears—anything but the red-faced rage that took possession of Lillith. As Tess watched in alarm, Lillith uttered a string of savage oaths, pried open the tape case and ripped the tape out, pulling it apart in pieces.

Tess gulped some air, then jumped back, her heart pounding in her chest, as she looked around wildly for a weapon, something to defend herself with if Lillith suddenly turned on her in that awful rage, the sort of rage that could easily lead to murder.

She could have just handed the killer the evidence against her, after virtually admitting that nobody else knew about the tape.

Strange, guttural grunts came from Lillith as she continued ripping up the tape.

Tess's gaze flew over the coffee table. Two magazines, a small rack of coasters, a ballpoint pen. Not exactly ammunition to stop a crazed killer. A porcelain Italian vase, which Tess used to hold pens and pencils, sat on the secretary near the door, but she would have to pass Lillith to get her hands on it. Then she saw the lamp on the side table.

Circling so that the sofa was between her and Lillith, Tess curled her fingers around the narrow end of the lamp base. A weapon of sorts, in case Lillith decided to dispose of Tess with the same vehemence with which she was shredding the videotape.

Having pulled all of the tape out, Lillith threw the

black plastic case to the floor and looked at Tess. Her eyes were glazed over. "She—will—not—destroy—my—marriage." Each word was sharp, emphatic, as if Lillith were shooting bullets from her mouth.

Tess searched frantically for calming words—words that would bring Lillith back to herself and get rid of the stranger who now faced her.

"Lillith—"

There was a banging on the apartment door. Never had a sound been so welcome to Tess.

"Lillith! Are you in there?" It was Rudy.

Tess released her grip on the lamp and dashed around the other end of the sofa to throw open the door.

Rudy stepped inside. "Oh, there you are, sweetheart. I looked for you in the suite and—Lillith, what's wrong?"

Lillith shook her head, as if throwing off a bad dream, and stared at the remnants of the tape she had just destroyed. The glaze was gone from her eyes and had been replaced by bewilderment, as if for one moment she didn't know how she had come to be in Tess's apartment with strings of black tape littering the carpet around her. Lillith's gaze flew to Tess and then to her husband, and she burst into tears.

Rudy gathered his wife's shuddering body into his arms. Glaring at Tess over Lillith's shoulder, he demanded, "This is outrageous! What have you done to her?"

"She—she's had a shock," Tess said lamely. And was *that* the understatement of the year!

"Here, sit down, darling," Rudy soothed, leading Lillith to the sofa and pushing her gently onto a cushion.

Her face buried in her hands, Lillith continued to weep great, wrenching sobs that seemed to come from the pit of her stomach and shook her body.

Tess didn't know what to do. Rudy sat down beside his wife and put his arm around her. "There, there, my darling. Please don't cry. Nothing can be as bad as all that."

Water, Tess thought, for lack of a better idea. She

hurried to the kitchen and returned with a glass of water for Lillith. Rudy took it and, with his other hand, pried one of his wife's hands from her face, wrapping it around the glass. "Take a drink, love," he urged, guiding the glass to her mouth.

Lillith gulped the water and the sobbing subsided, but she still looked as if she could faint dead away any minute. She handed the glass back to Rudy and he deposited it on the coffee table.

"Don't hate me, Rudy," Lillith whimpered. "Please don't hate me. I can stand anything but that."

Rudy darted a stunned glance in Tess's direction. He looked as if he'd been kicked in the stomach. "I adore you, Lillith. You know that. I—" His gaze fell on the broken tape case, which lay near his foot. "What's this?" Picking it up, he read the label. "*Barbie's Playhouse*? Barbie—that's what Heather called you."

Lillith started crying again, jerking out words between sobs. "I—I never—wanted you—to know. I was—young and naive—I thought—" Suddenly, she grabbed the tape case from Rudy's hands and held it clutched against her side. "I know that's no excuse. I thought I could use this disgusting film as a stepping stone to respectable acting jobs. I—oh, I was so stupid!"

Rudy's normally robust color had been replaced by a pasty gray. "You made a porn film?"

"I was only eighteen!" Lillith cried. "You hate me now, don't you? I disgust you. You want a divorce."

Rudy stood and backed away from the sofa. In his face, Tess could see his mind working it all out. Then, instead of responding to his wife, he turned on Tess. "How dare you shove this tape in my wife's face! Where did you get it?"

So, Tess was to be the scapegoat. Well, she wasn't going to stand still for that! "Now, just a darn minute. The tape came for Heather. I was trying to help by warning Lillith that a story on her—uh, youthful indiscretion—was likely to appear in *The National Scoop*."

Lillith wailed like a cat with its foot caught in the door. "I'm sorry, Rudy! I would rather die than cause you such embarrassment. I thought it was behind me, that you'd never have to know." She let go of the tape case in order to clutch her head in both hands in a grip so tight it turned her fingers white. "I won't cause you any more heartache. I can go back to work. I don't want anything in the divorce."

Rudy pulled her to her feet, holding her by both arms. "Divorce? Who said anything about a divorce?"

"I wouldn't blame you for wanting to be rid of me, Rudy. When this comes out—oh, my God—Kent will find out!"

Rudy blanched. "Not necessarily. When would he have access to that tabloid?"

Maybe Kent would not see the tabloid article, but if he heard about it, he'd have no trouble getting his hands on a copy. As the two seemed to have forgotten her presence, Tess decided it wasn't her place to point this out.

Lillith was gazing at her husband with desperate hope. "I won't blame you if you don't want to stay married to me after this. I know I should have told you, but I was afraid you'd leave me."

Rudy wrapped his thick arms around her. "Damn that Brackland woman!" At least, his wrath had turned from Tess to Heather.

Lillith remained very still in his arms. Finally, Rudy cleared his throat roughly and said, "I can't imagine anything that would make me want a divorce, sweetheart. Certainly not this."

"Oh, Rudy, do you really mean it?" Lillith's voice was muffled against his shoulder.

Being a witness to this intimate scene was making Tess uncomfortable. But they seemed to have forgotten her. Leaving the room would only draw their attention.

"I mean it," Rudy assured his wife, "and I'm not in any position to judge you, anyway. There's something pretty awful that I've been keeping from you."

She lifted her head to gaze at him with a perplexed expression.

"From what Brackland said to me, I think she may be

planning to do a story on me, too—on my financial problems."

Lillith blinked at him. Her tears had stuck her eyelashes together in spikes. "What financial problems?"

Rudy heaved a sigh so heavy he might have been carrying a ton of rocks on his shoulders. Releasing Lillith, he sank down on the sofa. "The company's in trouble, Lillith. We're mortgaged to the hilt and California real estate values are in the cellar. My attorneys are urging me to file for bankruptcy. I'll have to cut staff to the bone, but even then I'm not sure I can salvage the company."

"Oh, Rudy." Lillith sat down beside him and took his hand. "You've been dealing with this all by yourself and never said a word. You even let me spend all that money on the retreat."

He stared at her hand curled around his. "That's only a drop in the bucket, honey. And it's not just the company holdings I might lose. We'll probably have to sell our personal residences—all but one, anyway. The bankruptcy court can't take your domicile, but I don't think they'll let us keep four. You married a wealthy man, Lillith, and under the circumstances, I wouldn't blame you if you wanted out."

He finally lifted his head to look at his wife, his eyes full of such misery that Tess got a lump in her throat.

To Lillith's everlasting credit, she laughed and threw her arms around him. "I married you, sweetie, not your money! Who cares about all those houses? We can only live in one, anyway."

A tear actually rolled down Rudy's cheek. He tried to speak but couldn't.

Lillith stood and pulled him to his feet. "Let's go up to the suite." Like a sleepwalker, Rudy allowed himself to be led out of the apartment. "We'll start over together," Lillith said as she opened the door and guided him into the foyer. "I can take a few modeling jobs to help with expenses. We may have to send Kent to public school next year, but maybe that would be good for him."

"You really think we can start again?"

"I think we can do anything—together."

The door closed behind them and Tess sank weakly onto the nearest chair arm. Had she not witnessed the scene just played out in her sitting room, she would not have believed it. Lillith had undergone a transformation before Tess's eyes, from a raging stranger to a loving, supportive wife. It now appeared the marriage would survive, perhaps be stronger. With everything between them now out in the open, the Hansels could build their future together.

All very teary and romantic, but it didn't nullify the fact that both Rudy and Lillith had been desperate to keep the other from discovering what Heather Brackland was threatening to reveal. Both had feared that the other would want a divorce if the truth came out.

Two very good motives for murder.

Tess had never had any trouble picturing Rudy bringing that dumbbell down on Marcia Yoder's head. And after the side of Lillith she'd seen when she gave her the videotape, she no longer doubted that, pushed to the wall, Lillith could turn violent, too.

Tess gathered up the strips of videotape and its case and deposited them in the kitchen trash can, then checked her watch. The stock exchanges were closed on Saturday, and Luke should be up by now.

She needed to talk to him.

Chapter 28

Luke drove his Jaguar up to the bakery's drive-in window. "Give me a couple of old-fashioneds and a large coffee."

Tess had gotten him out of bed, after all, and he'd been dressed and in the car, without even a sip of coffee, before the last wisps of sleep left him. Now he said, "We'll go straight to Chief Butts from here."

Tess disagreed. "No. He's convinced Cail is the killer. He won't listen to my doubts unless I can give him evidence against somebody else."

"Honey, Butts is probably right."

"But what if he's wrong? Cail admitted to Lillith that he'd been selling illegal drugs in Victoria Springs, but he swore he didn't kill Marcia or poison Heather."

"Come on, love. Is he going to admit to murder when he hasn't even been arrested on that charge?"

The glass pane on the drive-up window slid to one side and a waitress handed out Luke's breakfast. He paid her, then set his coffee in a cup holder between the front seats and handed the small white sack to Tess. As he drove away from the window, Tess wrapped a napkin around one of the pastries and gave it to him.

Luke ate half the old-fashioned and washed it down with coffee. Watching him, Tess was struck again by how very handsome he was. She loved the clean lines of his nose and chin and the way that blond forelock fell across his forehead. And when he turned those blue eyes on her, she could get lost in them. Usually. But right now she was too impatient to dwell on Luke's many assets.

"I can't let this go until I'm sure Cail is the killer," she said, "instead of Lillith or Rudy or Pat."

Luke drove slowly through the business district, eating, drinking, and stopping for red lights. "Why is it *your* job to identify the murderer?" he asked mildly.

"Because, regardless of how much both of them irritated me, Marcia and Heather were my guests and Marcia had her skull bashed in my backyard! I'm too mad to let this go without trying to make a case against the killer." She raked her hands through her hair and frowned at Luke. "Chief Butts doesn't even have enough evidence to arrest Cail for Marcia's murder. And if Cail didn't do it, Butts has absolutely no evidence against anybody else—nor is he looking for any."

Luke popped the last of the first old-fashioned into his mouth and took a sip of coffee. "OK, how do you propose we go about getting evidence?"

"I'm thinking, I'm thinking," Tess mumbled.

Luke pulled over to the curb in front of a dress shop to finish his breakfast. "Let's go at this logically. Butts searched Cail's apartment, so we can assume there's no evidence against him except the fact that he got rid of a sack of rat poison."

"Which Lida says they had on hand because they had mice."

"Right. So for argument's sake, let's assume that Cail didn't kill Marcia or poison Heather." He ate the last of the pastry and settled back to finish his coffee.

"OK." Tess shifted sideways in her seat to face him. Bless him, he was going to help her. She could kiss him . . . but, no. That would merely distract him from the business at hand.

"If Cail didn't poison Heather, then the poison from his apartment is not the source of the arsenic. You don't have anything containing arsenic at Iris House. So where did Lillith or Rudy or Pat—or whoever—get the poison?"

"They couldn't have brought it with them," Tess mused, "because they couldn't have known that Heather was going to be here and that they'd want to kill her to keep her from writing stories about them. They had to buy the poison."

"Right." Luke drained his cup and started the engine. "How many places in town sell pesticides containing arsenic?"

"The two nurseries," Tess said. "The drug stores, the hardware stores. Maybe even the two supermarkets."

Luke pulled away from the curb. "We'll start with the drugstore on the next block."

More than two hours later, Tess and Luke had visited every store in town which they thought might sell pesticides. Both the town's drugstores checked their inventory of pesticides and rodent poisons. One had not sold any recently. The manager of the other drugstore could remember selling two sacks of rat poison during the last week, one to an elderly widow he'd known all his life, the other to a youngish woman who had a toddler in tow.

The nurseries were both on the outskirts of town, and they sold pesticides and rodent poisons regularly. Nobody on duty at either nursery could give a description of recent buyers, however.

Although Tess and Luke found rat poison in the supermarkets, the clerks on duty could not remember selling any within the past few weeks. Nor could they say with any certainty that they hadn't. One of them even called two other day clerks who were off work, but neither could recall selling any rat poison recently. A lot of people passed through their stations, they said, and the supermarkets were open twenty-four hours a day. The night shift clerks might have sold pesticides, but Luke and Tess would have to question them after they came on duty.

Tess didn't think any of her guests had gone to a supermarket at night. Only the Hansels had access to a car, which they'd rented at the Springfield airport. The other guests depended on Lida for transportation. By the same reasoning, she thought it unlikely that anybody had managed to get to the outskirts of town to one of the nurseries.

Somebody could have walked to a store, of course, but they'd have done it during the day, probably during one of the breaks. Which meant the store would have to be close enough to Iris House for somebody to walk there and back in half an hour.

That narrowed it down to two hardware stores and a small neighborhood grocery.

They discarded the idea that the killer had used a spray can to add poison to Heather's dinner. Nobody would be stupid enough to pull out a can of pesticide in front of their tablemates and a restaurant full of diners. That left poisoned powder.

After talking to the managers of all three stores within walking distance of Iris House, Tess made a list of customers who'd bought rodent poison within the last week—the ones their informants could remember well enough to describe, anyway.

Her list read as follows:

Middle-aged, heavy-set man with dark hair.

That could describe Rudy Hansel, except that his hair was more gray than dark, and when pressed, the hardware clerk thought the man was at least six feet tall. Rudy was only about five foot nine. The clerk allowed as how the guy could have been shorter than six feet, after all, but he couldn't swear to any of it.

Man in his twenties or early thirties. Slender, dark hair.

Could describe Cail, though the clerk didn't recall the man being particularly muscular. And besides, Cail wouldn't have needed to buy poison, since he had some in his apartment.

Edith Mallory, a retired school teacher in her seventies.

Tess only added this one to the list for the sake of thoroughness.

Two fortyish women of average weight and height.

The clerk could remember no more than this about the two customers, who had come in at different times during the last week. They could be any of hundreds of women in Victoria Springs, even Pat Snell (Tess could not get used to thinking of her as Dr. Patrice.) Lida, too, could fit such a vague description, though she already had access to rat poison at the center. Unless she didn't know Cail had taken it to his apartment, couldn't find it, and stopped to buy more. A very distant possibility, Tess thought, as Lida's motive for wanting Heather out of the way was far less compelling than the Hansels's or Pat's.

Nobody remembered selling poison to anybody who fit Lillith's description. And as one man told Tess when she described Lillith, "I'd have remembered that one if I'd waited on her." However, another said he saw so many people in a day that, during his busiest hours, he probably wouldn't notice if Kim Basinger walked up to his counter.

They'd talked to numerous sales people and had gathered very little relevant information as a result. Tess was discouraged. "Let's go back to your house," she said. "I need to pick up my car and collect Heather."

Chapter 29

Heather's return to Iris House was not exactly greeted with open arms. The other guests were having a discussion in the parlor when Tess and Heather walked in.

"Hi everybody," Heather called. "I'll be down to join you in a few minutes."

"Take your time," Rudy muttered.

Lillith and Pat gazed mutely at Heather. Neither look was welcoming.

"Oh, Pat," Heather said, "while I was in the hospital, I almost remembered where I've seen you before. It was right there on the edge of my memory, but I lost it. Never mind, it will come to me."

"Go to hell," Pat snarled. The thick venom startled Heather, who actually stepped back.

"We'll start our aerobics session in a few minutes, Heather," Lida said. "You can join us for that."

Heather nodded and climbed the stairs as Dorinda came down. "I finally heard from Chief Butts, Tess," Dorinda said. "I'm taking Marcia home tomorrow."

"Good," Tess said. "I know what a relief it must be to finally start putting all this behind you."

"If only the police had arrested Cail for Marcia's murder. Lida says they're sending him to California to face lesser charges there."

"Give it a little time. Chief Butts hasn't yet given up on making a murder charge stick."

Dorinda's murmured agreement did not sound very hopeful. She went on into the parlor, where the guests were rearranging the furniture to make room for the aerobics session. After Heather joined them, there was no conversation. Taped music and Lida's brief commands were the only sounds from the parlor. Tess retired to her apartment where, after scanning again the notes she'd made during her and Luke's questioning of sales clerks, she crumpled the paper and tossed it into a wastebasket.

The only thing accomplished by the two hours of questioning was that Tess had satisfied herself there was no blatant evidence in the murder investigation yet to be discovered. It was time, she decided, to leave it to Chief Butts to pursue a case against Cail.

Next morning a squabble between Heather and Rudy Hansel broke out over breakfast in the guest dining room. It seemed to be over whether the public had a right to know everything about a person's private life. Rudy was advocating that the right of privacy should take precedence and Heather, of course, disagreed— loudly.

Gertie didn't work on Sundays, so Tess had served bran flakes and strawberries to the guests. Lida would be taking them out for lunch *and* dinner today.

Now, as Tess was having a bowl of cereal at the table in the kitchen, she began to wish that Heather had not come back to Iris House. Mealtime had been more tranquil while she was gone. Now that she was back, almost everything she said seemed to irritate at least one of the other guests. And there was another week of the retreat to get through, for all except Dorinda, who was leaving today. From what Dorinda had said, she would never have come in the first place if Marcia hadn't insisted. If only Dorinda had talked her out of it, Marcia would still be alive.

Tired of hearing her guests' childish quarrels, Tess finished her cereal and left the kitchen with a big mug of coffee. She wanted to relax without interruption for a half-hour and decided the library in the tower was the best place to find the peace and quiet she longed for.

As she passed the Arctic Fancy Room, she noticed the door was ajar. Dorinda was folding clothes and placing them in a suitcase that lay open on the bed.

Dorinda looked up and smiled, and Tess paused at the door to ask, "Is Lida taking you to the Springfield airport?" Dorinda had come to Tess's apartment to take care of her bill last night.

Dorinda shook her head. "I'm riding in the limousine with Marcia." She glanced at her watch. "They're picking me up in a half-hour."

"Is there anything I can do to help you?"

"No, thanks."

Tess lifted her coffee mug. "I'm going up to the library for some quiet time then."

"I'll say goodbye before I leave," Dorinda said.

Tess climbed the wrought-iron spiral staircase to the third floor tower where she sank gratefully onto a pink, purple, and green floral chintz cushion. Ordinarily she presided at Sunday afternoon teas for her guests in the library and would now be preparing for that. But Lida had nixed any such idea for the retreat registrants. "They aren't allowed enough calories for snacks," Lida had said.

Which was fine with Tess. As Luke planned to catch up on some record-keeping this morning and would come over when he was finished, she looked forward to a quiet, restful time on her own.

Settling back into a corner of the white wicker sofa to finish her coffee, she thought fondly of childhood visits to her Aunt Iris and this house. The turret room had always fascinated her. She scanned the four sections of shelves which faced the curving, floor-to-ceiling windows, looking for a book in which she could lose herself for an hour or so.

As her gaze ran over the nonfiction section, she noticed that a slim volume had been placed flat on top of a row of books. Somebody had evidently taken it out and hadn't bothered replacing it in its proper place. Setting her coffee down, she went over to the bookshelf and pulled the book out. It was a history of Missouri published in the 1940s—one of the books which had belonged to Tess's Aunt Iris, who had been something of an authority on the state's history. She knew right where it belonged, on the bottom shelf.

Bending down to replace the book, she realized that there was no space for it. Odd. This book had resided in its place in the center of the bottom shelf since Tess had had the house remodeled as a bed and breakfast. She tried to make room for it, but could not push the other books apart enough to insert the history text.

Bother. Somebody had probably misshelved a book. She laid the history down on the floor and ran her fingers along book spines, looking for the book that was out of place.

Every book had title and author's name printed on its spine, except for one. A red leather-bound book's spine was blank. Tess pulled it out and turned it over in her hand. Although there was a red satin ribbon bookmark protruding from the bottom, there was no printing on the cover anywhere. Tess looked at the first page and saw loopy, feminine handwriting. It seemed to be a journal or a diary, but Tess had never seen it before.

Frowning, she returned to the sofa, let the book fall open at random, and read:

Tuesday, March 2

I love our room at the B & B! The yard and gardens are beautiful, too. If only I didn't have to share this inspiring setting with D. I have given up trying to explain to her why truth is so important to me now. She says it's just nonsense that Ahmed has put into my head and that I can't put the toothpaste back in the tube.

Tess frowned at this phrase, having no idea what the writer was referring to. She continued reading.

She keeps going on about the statute of limitations, whatever that means. But I don't care about her legal mumbo-jumbo. I must sweep all falsehood out of my life. I've decided to try to find the judge who presided at the trial against the insurance company. I'll tell him I lied under oath and he can take whatever action he thinks is necessary. At least it will be off my conscience. D. says if I do, then I'll be implicating her, too, since she lied as well. I told her that's her problem, not mine.

Tess's frown had deepened as she read and tried to make sense of the words. Obviously this was Marcia Yoder's journal, the one Dorinda had been looking for in their room after Marcia's death. Gazing pensively out the window, Tess remembered Marcia coming to the apartment, the day before she died, to ask if she could spend her break in the library. Marcia had brought her journal with her, perhaps had written this last entry while there, but why had she left it behind, stuck in between two nonfiction books?

It appeared that Marcia had wanted to hide her journal. To keep Dorinda from reading it? And what was all that business about lying under oath?

The morning after Marcia's murder, when Tess had taken Dorinda's breakfast up to her room, hadn't Dorinda said something about an insurance company settlement? She'd been referring to the company that had insured the truck driver who broadsided the Fenster family car, killing Dorinda and Marcia's parents. And, from Marcia's journal entry, it sounded as if the sisters had had to take the company to court to get the money.

But what was the lie Marcia wrote about? It sounded serious since Dorinda had apparently worried about being implicated.

"Tess?"

Dorinda's voice behind her made Tess jump. She wore a light jacket over a brown polyester dress. The jacket had large, silvery buttons. Engrossed in her thoughts, Tess hadn't heard Dorinda come up the stairs.

"The limo is here," Dorinda said. "The driver is taking my suitcases out now. I wanted to—" She stopped abruptly and leaned over Tess's shoulder. "What's that?" Marcia's journal still lay open on Tess's lap.

Tess closed the journal quickly and stood. "Nothing."

Dorinda stared at her.

"That's my sister's journal! I recognize her handwriting."

Tess managed a smile. "It was on the bottom shelf. Apparently Marcia put it there and forgot about it."

Dorinda had walked around the sofa now and, before Tess knew what she was about, she snatched the journal from Tess's hand and opened it to the last page, the one Tess had read.

"I was about to bring it down to you," Tess said, trying to sound casual—trying to sound as if she hadn't read Marcia's words and begun to put a few pieces of the puzzle together. Trying to hide the fact that a horrifying conclusion was taking shape in her mind.

Dorinda closed the journal. "My sister wrote the most ridiculous nonsense in her journal." Her voice was steady, but her eyes fixed on Tess were calculating, as if she were wondering how much Tess had read, how much she knew. Tess could easily imagine Dorinda sizing up a hostile witness in court with just that look.

Tess felt her throat tighten and she couldn't keep the words back. "It's hardly nonsense. The two of you lied to get money from an insurance company."

Dorinda continued to assess her for a long moment, then said coldly, "They could afford it. The money didn't come out of the driver's pocket. He lost his job, but I'm sure he found another."

"So the money to go to law school . . ."

"You don't understand, Tess. I could not have gone to school otherwise. My parents' estate amounted to a few thousand dollars, after all the bills were paid. The money from the insurance company allowed me to keep Marcia with me and saw us through my three years of law school. I always looked at it as a fair exchange for the loss of our parents."

"But Marcia didn't see it that way."

Dorinda's mouth twisted. "That's why I came to this stupid retreat. I thought I could change her mind."

"But you couldn't . . ."

"It wasn't going to change *her* life, going to the judge, but it was going to destroy mine. I was talking to my mother, Tess. I only looked away for a minute—and the light changed."

Tess was beginning to understand. "You were driving, and you ran a red light. You caused the accident that killed your parents."

"Don't you think I've suffered years of guilt over that? I had nightmares for months afterward. It's not as if I took a gun and shot them, Tess. I loved my parents, but I couldn't see any reason why Marcia and I should struggle to make ends meet for the rest of our days because of one mistake that anybody could have made." She sounded so reasonable. She must have used the same rationalizations on herself and Marcia many times before.

"So you testified that the other driver ran the red light, and you got Marcia to say that, too."

To Dorinda, the end had justified the means. It was a fair bargain all the way around, never mind that the other driver had lost his job.

"Insurance companies pay settlements all the time," Dorinda said. "They budget for it. It's part of the cost of doing business."

Briefly Tess glanced toward the window that looked down on the backyard. "That night, when Marcia went out in the rain to dance, I heard her leaving your room. I heard you say, 'Don't do this, Marcia.' " Tess took a step away. "I assumed you were trying to talk her out of going out in the rain. But that wasn't it, was it? You were begging her not to expose the lie you'd both told." As Tess edged toward the door, Dorinda moved to block her way.

"Almost twenty years ago!" Dorinda spat out. "After all that time, she wanted to cleanse her damned conscience! But I was the one who was going to pay for it. I would have lost my job."

"Like the truck driver," Tess said softly.

Dorinda brushed this away with a shake of her head. "I could very well have been disbarred. I tried to tell her, but she didn't care! After all the sacrifices I'd made for her, she didn't *care*!"

Tess understood it all now, every ugly bit. "There was no case of mistaken identity," she said. "The night Marcia was killed, you knew she was wearing Heather's raincoat."

Dorinda studied her for a long moment. "I followed her to the stairs," she said finally. "She didn't hear me. I stood at the top and watched her put on the raincoat and go out."

Tess stared at the shiny buttons on Dorinda's jacket. Light reflecting off them at night would have produced a flash—the sparkle Donnie Armory had seen. "And you picked up a dumbbell from the sitting room and followed her." Tess took a step toward the door, but Dorinda didn't move.

"I only meant to talk to her again."

"Then why take the dumbbell?"

"I wasn't thinking straight," Dorinda snapped. "But when I saw her—I realized talking would do no good. We committed fraud, Tess. Marcia was only a child, but I was an adult. I couldn't let her expose me."

"What about Heather?" Dorinda's calm, cold reason sent a chill through Tess. "You sat beside Heather at dinner the night she became ill. You must have bought the rat poison and put it in her food." The absence of denial was admission enough for Tess. "Why, Dorinda? I don't understand why you poisoned Heather."

"I wanted to be sure the police continued to think Heather was the intended victim. I was careful not to add enough to her food to kill her, just enough so they'd realize she'd been poisoned."

Tess took a step back and Dorinda pressed forward. As Tess took another step back, Dorinda said, "No one else has to know this, Tess. Cail is a known drug dealer.

We'll be doing the world a favor to get him off the street for good."

Tess halted. There was no escape behind her. "I'll think it over, Dorinda. Now, please let me pass." Dorinda didn't move. "Step back or I'll scream loud enough for the whole house to hear."

From far away, Tess heard somebody calling her name. One of the guests was looking for her. Thank God!

To Tess's vast relief, Dorinda stepped to one side— to let her leave the library, or so Tess thought. But instead, Dorinda grabbed a bronze iris statuette which sat on a shelf near the door.

Dorinda had already lifted the statuette above her head in both hands when Tess comprehended her intention and scrambled aside. But not quickly enough. Dorinda brought the statuette down in a glancing blow to the side of Tess's head, and everything went black.

Tess came back to consciousness, turned her head, and groaned. She squinted at the light pouring in through floor-to-ceiling windows. She was lying on the floor of the library.

What . . . ? How . . . ? It all came rushing back.

A sharp pain stabbed the side of Tess's head as she struggled to a sitting position. But Dorinda was gone. She had to stop her.

Slowly, she pushed herself to her feet. Swaying back and forth, she waited for the pain to subside a little. Then, bracing herself against the wall, she made her way to the stairs and descended, hanging on to the wrought-iron railing. Pain stabbed at her temple with each step.

The upstairs hall seemed to be a mile long. Tess wasn't sure she could make it all the way down to the first floor without stopping to rest. She had reached the Arctic Fancy Room. The door was still open. She caught hold of the door facing to steady herself. Dorinda and her suitcases were gone.

Tess stumbled to the bed and picked up the phone on the bedside table. With trembling fingers, she dialed.

Butts answered.

"Chief Butts, this is Tess Darcy." Her voice shook.

"You sound funny, Tess. What's wrong?"

Tess took a deep breath. "I know who killed Marcia Yoder and it wasn't Cail Hurst."

Chapter 30

Chief Butts stood just inside the parlor door. Luke had arrived at Iris House an hour ago, summoned by a phone call from Tess. She had managed to reassure Luke that she had a tender bump on the side of her head, but otherwise she was all right. Then the two of them had interrupted the guests' support session so that Tess could fill them in on what had happened in the library. Tess had just finished when Butts arrived.

"Good thing you got to a phone as quick as you did, Tess," Butts said.

Tess showed admiral restraint in not reminding him that he'd been telling her to butt out all week.

"I saw Dorinda leave," Lida said breathlessly. "I was looking for Tess and Dorinda came down the stairs. She said Tess wasn't around, that she thought she'd gone out. I believed her. I just stood there and let her go."

"Just as well you didn't try to stop her," Butts said, "considering what she did to Tess. Fortunately, we intercepted the funeral home's limousine en route to Springfield."

"Yes, thank goodness."

Butts peered more closely at Tess. "You sure you're OK?"

"I'm fine."

Butts leaned against the door frame. "Miz Brackland, you won't have to worry about being poisoned again, now that we've got Fenster in custody."

"I wasn't worried before," Heather said. "You said it was Cail who poisoned my food."

Butts ducked his head and shifted his weight from one foot to the other. He opened his mouth, then evidently lost his train of thought and coughed loudly. Tess took pity on him.

"We all thought it was Cail."

"Even I didn't believe him when he swore he didn't do it," Lida said.

"He sure acted like the guilty party," Butts inserted. "Getting rid of that sack of rat poison like he did. But if you hadn't seen him do that, Tess, we wouldn't have picked him up and turned him over to the California authorities. He could've got clean away again."

A second compliment—sort of. Would wonders never cease?

"Thank goodness you took him in before he had a chance to get out of town," Tess said.

Butts's ruddy face twisted into a real smile. "I just thought I'd let you know we got Fenster. She hasn't said a word, o'course, except to ask for an attorney. Lawyers." He shook his head. "Too smart to talk to the police."

"Well, she sure talked to me," Tess said. "She came to the retreat with Marcia to talk her out of exposing the lie she told under oath years ago—the lie that provided Dorinda with the money to support the two of them while she finished law school. It was all there in Marcia's journal."

"We got the journal in the evidence locker," Butts said. "That, along with Tess's testimony, is gonna put Fenster in jail for a long, long time."

"That night when Dorinda killed Marcia, she finally realized she couldn't talk Marcia out of making a clean breast of it. Marcia was going to the authorities. Dorinda knew the only way to keep her quiet was to kill her. Oh, and, Chief, you should probably take a photograph of

Dorinda to that little neighborhood grocery store on Redbud Avenue," Tess said. "The manager there said that two fortyish women had purchased rat poison from his store in the past week. I'd almost bet one of them was Dorinda. Of course, Dorinda will have gotten rid of the rest of the poison by now. She told me she didn't intend to kill Heather with it. She just wanted to make sure you kept thinking Heather was the intended victim."

Butts surveyed her with interest. "So you questioned store clerks about the poison? Can't resist conducting your own investigation, can you, Tess?"

She started to bristle. How could he think of criticizing her when she'd just turned over Marcia Yoder's murderer to him? "Good thing I did, too."

Butts let that pass.

"So when Marcia hid her journal to keep her sister from confiscating it, I guess it never occurred to her that Dorinda would do much worse than that."

"Marcia always seemed to be out in left field somewhere," Lillith added. "She didn't see things, even her own sister, the way other people did."

"I'm sure she couldn't imagine that the sister who'd always taken care of her would turn on her," Tess mused. "If only she hadn't trusted Dorinda so much . . ."

"I have to get back to the station," Butts said and stuck out his hand. Tess shook it. "We'll need to get a statement from you, Tess, but tomorrow will be soon enough."

When Tess and Luke were back in the apartment, Pat tapped on the door and stuck her head in. "Can I have a word?"

"Sure," Tess said, gesturing her in.

Pat closed the door behind her. "I wanted to tell you, Tess, that I decided to take your advice." She shrugged. "I really have no choice but to make the best of a bad situation. Tomorrow I'll call the radio station and have them tape a statement from me. I'm going to tell my listeners that I can now understand their weight problems much better than before because I've been there. But I'm dealing with it, and they can, too. I only hope I can convince them of my sincerity."

"I'm glad to hear that, Pat. I'll bet your audience will grow even bigger, once the word gets out."

"I'll have to work hard to change my image. I'm going to share with them some of the low-calorie meals we've had here, and ask them to share their own recipes and weight-loss secrets." She looked thoughtful.

"Sharing recipes sounds like a good idea," Tess said.

Pat nodded. "It might even turn into a newsletter. Subscriptions should pour in." She chuckled. "Good God, I could turn into one of those happy homemakers you see on TV. But, as I said, what else can I do?"

More income for Dr. Patrice. She hadn't really changed all that much. Tess and Luke exchanged a glance of mutual understanding.

"And," Pat said, "I'm going to take the wind out of Heather's sails, too. She still hasn't figured out who I am, but on the last day of the retreat I'm going to reveal my identity to everybody." She grinned in anticipation of the event. "The radio station will have aired my tape by then, and Heather's scoop will have been pulled out from under her. Even if the tabloid runs the story anyway, it won't do much damage."

When Pat left, Tess turned to Luke. "I only wish I could derail Heather's stories on the Hansels, as well. But at least Rudy and Lillith seem to be dealing with it, so tabloid stories will have little effect on their relationship. That doesn't mean they won't be hassled by reporters, though."

"It'll be a three-day wonder, sweetheart." Luke took her hand and pulled her down with him on the couch. "The news hounds will be on to something else before you know it."

"Do you really think so?"

"I'm sure of it. Besides, you can't make everybody in the world happy, Tess."

"I'm only concerned about my little corner of the world."

He put his arms around her and drew her close. "Glad to hear it, my love. You can start with me."

ORANGE FRENCH TOAST
Serves 1

¼ cup skim milk
3 tablespoons fat-free egg substitute
1 teaspoon vanilla extract
Dash cinnamon
2 slices reduced-calorie whole wheat bread
¼ cup nonfat vanilla yogurt
4 sections from peeled and sectioned navel orange

In a bowl, combine milk, egg substitute, vanilla, and cinnamon. Dip bread slices in egg mixture, coating both sides.

Spray nonstick skillet with nonstick cooking spray. Heat. Add bread slices. Cook on medium heat until browned on one side. Turn and brown other side.

Cut French toast slices diagonally in half. Arrange in fan on plate and top with yogurt. Garnish with orange slices.

250 calories, 2 grams fat

VEGETABLE-CHEESE QUICHE
Serves 6

1 tablespoon margarine
4 cups broccoli flowerets
1 large onion, chopped
1 cup sliced fresh mushrooms
1 cup all-purpose flour
1 tablespoon baking powder
1 cup fat-free egg substitute
1 cup skim milk
2 cups shredded nonfat mozzarella cheese

Preheat oven to 350 degrees. Spray 9-inch pie pan with nonstick cooking spray.

Melt margarine in nonstick skillet. Add broccoli, onion, and mushrooms. Cook, stirring constantly until softened, about 15 minutes.

In a large bowl, combine flour and baking powder. Add egg substitute and milk. Mix until smooth. Stir in cheese and broccoli mixture. Spoon into pie pan. Bake until top is golden and knife inserted in center comes out clean, about 35 minutes.

229 calories, 3 grams fat per serving

MEXICAN OMELET
Serves 4

1 onion, chopped
¼ cup jalapeno peppers, finely chopped
1 tomato, diced
½ teaspoon dried oregano
2 cups fat-free egg substitute
⅓ cup shredded, reduced-fat Monterey Jack cheese
¼ cup mild salsa

Spray a medium nonstick skillet with nonstick cooking spray. Heat. Add onion and pepper. Cook, stirring as needed until softened, about 5 minutes. Add tomato and oregano. Cook, stirring as needed, until tomato is softened, about 2 minutes.

Meanwhile, spray a large nonstick skillet with nonstick cooking spray. Place over medium-low heat. Add the egg substitute and cook until set, about 8 minutes, lifting edges frequently with a spatula to let the uncooked egg substitute flow underneath.

When egg substitute is set, sprinkle evenly with tomato mixture, salsa, and cheese. Cook, covered, until cheese is melted, about 3 minutes. Serve immediately.

112 calories, 2 grams fat per serving

OVEN FRIED CHICKEN
Serves 2

2 3-ounce boneless, skinless chicken breasts
½ cup skim milk
½ cup cornflakes, crushed
Dash pepper
Paprika

Dip chicken in milk. Coat both sides with cornflake crumbs. Season with pepper and sprinkle with paprika.

Bake at 400 degrees for 30 minutes. Reduce heat to 350 degrees. Cover loosely with foil and bake 20 to 30 minutes longer, until chicken is done.

210 calories, 3 grams fat per serving

FISH NUGGETS WITH
LEMON TARTAR SAUCE
Serves 2

*½ pound skinless halibut fillets or other white fish
fillets*
¼ cup nonfat egg substitute
1 tablespoon skim milk
2 tablespoons grated Parmesan cheese
¼ cup cornflake crumbs
¼ teaspoon paprika
¼ cup fat-free mayonnaise
1 tablespoon finely chopped dill pickle
1 teaspoon finely shredded lemon peel
½ teaspoon lemon juice

Preheat oven to 450 degrees. Rinse fish and pat dry.
Cut into 12 bite-sized pieces. Set aside.

In medium bowl, combine egg substitute and skim
milk. In large plastic bag, combine Parmesan cheese,
cornflake crumbs, and paprika. Add fish chunks to egg
substitute mixture. Coat well and remove fish from mixture. Place fish in plastic bag with crumb mixture. Seal
bag and toss until fish is coated.

Arrange fish in a single layer on a baking sheet or
shallow baking pan. Bake about 5 minutes or until fish
flakes easily with fork.

Meanwhile, stir together mayonnaise, pickle, lemon
peel, and lemon juice. Serve fish with the lemon tartar
sauce.

191 calories, 3 grams fat per serving

Discover Murder and Mayhem with

∾ Southern Sisters Mysteries ∾

by

ANNE GEORGE

MURDER ON A BAD HAIR DAY

78087-9/$6.50 US/$8.50 Can

MURDER ON A GIRLS' NIGHT OUT

78086-0/$6.50 US/$8.50 Can

MURDER RUNS IN THE FAMILY

78449-1/$6.50 US/$8.50 Can

MURDER MAKES WAVES

78450-5/$6.50 US/$8.50 Can

MURDER GETS A LIFE

79366-0/$6.50 US/$8.50 Can

And in Hardcover

MURDER SHOOTS THE BULL

97688-9/$22.00 US/$32.00 Can